Withered Zion

William LJ Galaini

"You know that among the Gentiles those whom they recognize as their rulers lord it over them, and their great ones are tyrants over them. But it is not so among you; but whoever wishes to become great among you *must* be your servant, and whoever wishes to be first among you *must* be slave of all."

Christ Jesus ~ Mark 10: 42-44 (NRSV)

I

Charles Mueller

Dear Lord, I have come to doubt of late whether or not you hear my prayers. Too many monsters hold office and I am no match for them. I am too faint of heart and lack the personal courage to fight. Evil thrives when good men do nothing, and I have certainly done nothing.

I deserve no place in your heavenly kingdom. I deserve no forgiveness even though I am certain you would grant it warmly if I asked. I do not take this, my last moment on your Earth, to ask . . . but to pray.

Our Father, who art in heaven, hallowed be thy name. Forgive the citizens, most of which only obey the state out of fear. Forgive the children who are raised thinking that they are better than the rest of the world. Forgive those who mock and harm and hunt the atheists, the homosexuals, the unstately, the deviants, and the strange. Forgive those who create and propogate the laws to permit such heinous acts. Forgive the monsters, who play as men of faith while desecrating your land on Earth. Forgive those who disregard sacrifice, temperance and all other virtues that are required of piety.

Forgive the people of the United States of Christendom. Forgive them when they stand before your only son to be judged.

With that, I thank you Lord. I thank you for my childhood and for my life and my freedom of choice. I should not have squandered them so.

We will not speak again.

II

Thomas Hung

It happened at church, just after the Easter service. I was sifting through the exiting crowd on the reluctant hunt for Anne and her parents. Per usual, I had skipped the service despite being prominent enough in the right circles to warrant a weekly seat at the National Cathedral. It seemed like a waste of a productive Sunday to me.

There they were. Anne was pretty as always, chatting with some friends whose names I forgot. Her parents stood vigilant at the top of the steps, her mother's hands folded into her father's elbow like the perfect, happy Sunday couple.

My game face was on. I was just climbing the steps against the crowd when the distinct crack of a pistol went off. The echoing report made everyone dive to the ground as soon as their bodies caught up with their senses. Everyone dove, that is, except for me. I'm not sure why, but I've just always had an emotional distance from what happens around me. Perhaps that is the secret to being a good federal journalist. You have to be detached.

Scanning for the source of the sound, I turned just in time to see Secretary of Christendom Charles Mueller's knees buckle. I watched his body tumble down the steps and flop onto the sidewalk; arms and legs strewn, his lifeless eyes focused up toward the sky. I didn't realize it at the time, but I was the first one to rush to his side. My body just carried me there, and brought me to my knees next to him, his hand in mine. It was clear to me that he had shot himself despite someone in the crowd shouting 'assassination!'

Thinking back on it, the gun's report was almost comical. There was a hollow ring to it instead of the deep gravity one might expect of such a world-altering thing as a bullet. Macabre though it was his tumble down the stairs and flop on the pavement could have been accompanied by a laugh track. Anne's parents said it was God's work that Mueller landed near my feet after his thumping journey down the cathedral steps, but I suspect that was just their sycophancy talking. Insensitive as it was to imagine adding a laugh track to a man's suicide, someone thinking that *I* could be involved in God's plan was truly callous. Besides, I had only been a bystander to a good man's suicide. I was a passenger of history, at least for the time being.

I hadn't noticed them in my prior meetings with Mueller, but he had beautiful eyes. They were vibrant and younger than the rest of his face, and in their reflection I could vividly see the clouds. As cliché as it was, I covered his eyelids with my hands and guided them downward. It was all I could think of to do for a dead man.

Within what seemed moments, the tall black tractor trailers of Civil Seraphim pulled up, curved themselves into a shielding semi-circle, and closed everyone in who hadn't fled the scene. The American flag, stripes of red and white with the radiant cross where stars once were, dominated our eyes as black SUV's swarmed around us. Out spilled Civil Seraphim, some in armor, some in suits, but all armed. A few people seemed nervous but most held either high station or considerable popularity and weren't overly concerned. No one should need to be driven off or privately interrogated and besides, it was *obvious*. The Secretary had shot himself in the temple just as he was exiting the National Cathedral after service.

He had shot himself... I think on it now but at the time I was rearranging my day in my head as though an inconvenience had cropped up like a flat tire or a sudden cancellation. Everyone else had taken out their planners to frantically email people, or turn to each other in an effort to get whatever story they felt they needed for Civil Seraphim straight.

"I didn't see a gunman, did you? Are we safe?"

"I think the shooter's gone."

"Didn't he shoot himself?"

"Why would he shoot himself?"

I, of course, was on the phone with my boss in a heartbeat. A finger in one ear, my phone in the other, I paced up and down the church steps until I got him on the line, occasionally glancing over my shoulder to look at Mueller's body under someone's dress coat. He looked like a homeless man napping on the mall lawn with everyone mulling around him, ignoring his plight.

"What happened!?" Robert Koss, my editor-in-chief, yelped in my ear over the phone so loudly it made the speaker crackle. Someone must have already called him. How absurd was that?

"The Secretary of Christendom came right out on the front steps of the National Cathedral after service, put a pistol to his head, and shot himself!" I shouted back, already working the headline. The din around me was getting louder and I found myself retreating from the chattering crowd.

"Is Seraph there?"

"Yeah, but they're not telling us much. They haven't

told me not to talk to anyone yet." In fact they hadn't told us anything at all, as they were still busy putting up barricades.

"Well, they're going to have to come out with some kind of statement, and *soon*. I just got a call from The News and they were wondering what the word was."

"I don't know... I don't know..." I replied, trying to figure out what the Civil Seraphim would do for an official statement.

"Did, uh... did the Secretary really just put a gun to his head and shoot himself?" Robert sounded a little shaken. Secretary Mueller had held office for nearly two decades and had maintained a high level of popularity. He was an everyman, and made prayer seem like a birthright for everyone to exercise. Something about him made you feel safe, and deserving of God's love. I had met him only twice, but he remembered me the second time. I liked him, and I always looked forward to reporting on his doings.

I sighed. "Yes. Yes he did."

"Think he left a note?"

"If he did we'll never see it."

There was a long silence. "Okay." Robert started. "You'll write three versions of the cover story. One will be assassination. Another will be unknown cause of death awaiting the autopsy. And the third will be suicide, but leave that one loose because we'll need to plug in the motivation and details once Seraph gives them to us. I'll try and get on the phone with the Vice President. See if he approves of any of the angles. When you're finished there get cracking."

"Alright. Sounds like a plan. I'll have them all ready by midnight for the morning edition."

And with that I hung up. I looked about and

watched everyone else. Perhaps I was trying to see how I was expected to behave. Maybe I was one of the few witnesses impatient for Civil Seraphim to get my questioning over with, since so many others seemed like they were anxious. The other bystanders stood in small clumps, chatting wildly and holding each other. What a good ice-breaker the public death of a man must be. What good networking it must provide.

"We must ask you who you were on the phone with." A body-armored Civil Seraphim soldier appeared out of nowhere behind me, his mask and helmet hanging on his belt. His face was surprisingly young for a voice so stern. I wasn't used to seeing them with their masks off. The thought occurred to me that he perhaps was trying to be less intimidating given the privilege of the crowd that frequents the National Cathedral in the North East of Washington DC: diplomats, politicians, military leaders, and industry captains.

"My name is Thomas Hung from the Christendom Post. I was on the phone with my editor-in-chief Robert Koss." I handed him my cell and with a sharp, practiced motion he pulled a cord from his sleeve and plugged it into my phone, downloading its history and contents. After a moment he was done, and handed it back to me.

"We must question you. Please report to truck two." he said. Then he stepped past me to the next nearby person.

The tractor-trailers were parked at the front of the church in a semi-circle like wagons protecting the women and children in an old western, a third one now added to the ranks, in an effort to obscure the scene from the rest of the street. Each trailer was black with a colorfully painted billowing American flag; Christ's cross bold and bright where the fifty stars once shined. The trucks themselves were armored with glossy reinforced panels, their wheels coming up to my shoulder. I found my assigned truck, and walked up the appropriate ramp into its side. I seemed to be among the first to arrive since there was no line. Inside was a series of high cubicles, each with sliding curtains that clanked like a communal shower. An armed Civil Seraphim, this time with his dehumanizing helmet on and machinegun strapped downward on his chest, pointed me to the farthest curtain. "Head there, absolutely no talking to anyone unless spoken to by CS."

I did as I was told, slipped through the curtain into a dim space, and sat in a small chair. I rested my hands on the desk and noticed how they glowed under the light of the tiny affixed lamp. The uniformed woman across from me had a silver stylus out and scribbled away on her digital planner without looking at me. Her grey-streaked hair was wound tightly into a professional bun and her eyelids flicked about as she sorted through her materials. I must have been her first customer.

"What is your name?" she asked while using her planner to snap a photo of me.

"Mr. Thomas Hung."

"Are you a citizen?"

"Yes. Born in New Hampshire."

"Ethnicity?"

"Asian-American."

"Occupation."

"I am a journalist for the Christendom Post." Upon answering that one, I got some eye contact. She looked me over, leaned back in her chair out of direct light, and closed her folder containing the rest of the questions. Only her resting hand remained under the lamp's direct beam.

"What did you witness?" she asked.

"I heard the gunshot, turned, and saw Secretary Mueller rolling down the stairs. I went to his aid, but he was already dead."

"I saw you on the surveillance tape. Everyone but you ducked when the gunshot went off. What is your reason for that?" she asked before taking a sip of water.

"I'm not sure. I think I just couldn't believe someone would discharge a gun on the steps of our national church. Instinctively I thought of it more as a loud sound than an actual gun."

"Where on his body was he shot?"

"In the right temple."

"Did you see who shot him?"

I immediately saw where this was headed. "No. I didn't even see the gun, just him falling and rolling. I'm sorry. I wish I had."

That was pretty much it. I was reminded that I had to follow all federal journalistic regulations. After nodding several times in agreement, I walked through the exit in the back, headed down the ramp to the street, and found myself staring at a huge crowd. Hundreds of people had gathered, and the placed barriers were barely holding as they called out for Mueller and argued with police. I saw the occasional nightstick fly and smack a person down to the pavement.

"Do not disturb Civil Seraphim's investigation!" a loud speaker boomed. "Everything is under control. Please do not force us to disperse this crowd!" I was glad that I had permission to leave. I didn't want to see that happen.

It suddenly occurred to me that I should have caught up with Anne and her parents. I had actually completely forgotten about them. Lingering around for their examinations to be over didn't appeal to me though, and to be honest I suspected that Anne would somehow make a man's suicide about her and her trauma. I didn't have my game face ready to deal with her attention-grabbing. I was in no mood.

III

Thomas Hung

"They're going with assassination." I said as I
swung open Robert's office door.

"Are you sure?" he asked, eyes bleary and fingertips
rubbing his temples. He looked like more of a wreck than
usual. Funny. I saw a man shoot himself in the head and I
was comparatively fine.

"Oh yeah, I'm sure. Positive. They're fishing right
now for those who can confirm that he committed
suicide."

Robert went to a shade even paler than before.
"You...right over the phone told me he committed suicide!
You *told* me! If anyone was listening or monitoring then
not only *you* will be questioned but me too. They'll search
me-what were you..."

He was too scared to even finish his own sentences.
"Robert, your imagination is too active. They're not going
to give us a hard time. We're The Christendom Post! Us! I
wouldn't worry. Why would they bother us? We're on
the same side."

"Did you lie to them? About *anything?*" He was
getting a bit too frantic for my tolerance.

"You need to relax." I said, smirking at him while
flopping on his office couch.

The phone rang. Robert just blinked at it. I got up
and reached over his desk, lifting the receiver.

"Editor-in-Chief's office. Hung speaking." I

answered.

"I must speak to the editor-in-chief himself." the voice said. I held the phone out to Robert. He took it. I suppose lifting it from my hand instead of from the desk made it less threatening.

Clearing his throat, he answered, "This is Koss." He nodded eagerly while listening. "Uh-huh. Right. Right. Consider it done. No, not at all. Thank you so much. Yes. Thank you."

He hung up. "Assassination by an unidentified gunman. The footage has been on The News for ten minutes now." Robert lifted his TV remote. On came an anchor, flushed yet monotone. A frozen frame of footage displayed to the left of the anchor's head showed the image of a dark, blurry figure with an outstretched hand toward Mueller's head. The surveillance had been well altered, and the fictitious gunman looked completely natural.

"Authorities have released the photo of an Albert Sergent, a registered atheist that has been living in the D.C. area for over three years. He has no known alias. Albert Sergent is approximately five foot ten with brown eyes and hair. If you see him, do not attempt to apprehend him or speak with him because he is armed and extremely dangerous. Simply call 911."

A photo of a man came up, filling the screen. He seemed mousy and slightly vacant. Below his mug shot was a written stream of information listing his tattoos, scars, and a disfigured hand. A lost, miserable look filled his eyes as he stared out through the TV screen directly at me. They had obviously picked him solely for the photograph. Sergent was haunting.

"I'll get on this. But I've got to make a few phone

calls first for some more flesh on the story." I said. I had a hard time taking my eyes from this man's face.

The city coroner was a friend of mine, and we had shared many a basketball discussion over a corpse. Often I found myself in his morgue as I drilled him for whatever details he could disclose, and some he couldn't. Luckily I got him on my backup cell phone, while ducking into a storage closet down the hall.

"So, what you got?" I casually asked him the moment the phone answered.

"What?" he replied loudly. "I can't hear you. Who is this? Call back from a land line." And he hung up on me. I was puzzled, and began to dial him again when my cell rang. I answered. It was him from another line.

"His knees are worn like leather." He blurted without greeting or explanation. "He spent a lot of his time on his knees. He often wore them bloody." There was a long silence. I didn't know what to say. He had never been like this with me before. "Put that in your story." And he hung up.

I went to my office to see if any details had been faxed or phoned to me. So far all that had come in from Civil Seraphim was a list of what I wasn't allowed to type. Checking my voicemail I heard Anne's voice.

"Oh Tom! Who would do such a thing! God rest his kind soul. Are you okay? My parents saw you going into a trailer but they didn't see you come out. I hope everything's fine. Please call me as soon as you get this, okay? Please?" There was a long pause. Come on. Come on Anne. You know you feel obligated. Mommy and Daddy told you to say it… "I love you." She finally said right before hanging up.

They are so predictable. Anne is the naïve and

somewhat flakey daughter of a first generation industrialist who moved a textile business to the States from Vietnam. Being extremely wealthy wasn't enough to put them on the high society radar for some reason, so they trained her on me. Being a federal journalist, I know, or at least have access to, anyone in the capital. I'm an easy way for a chance meeting or a casual handshake to occur. They aren't dumb people, but neither am I. I'm drawing it out. If I'm that important to making the family business and name flourish stateside, it's going to be *my* family, damn it and *my* business. I'm going to run it. I'm just waiting for her father to offer me enough of his business upon wedlock to where I can get a foothold. In the interim, I balance things between 'playing it cool' and 'thinking about kids.'

I sat down at my computer, which I keep unplugged most of the time for privacy, and got ready to type. This is how I write:

The process begins when there is a need. A need for a story. Details are often given to Robert or sometimes even to me directly by Civil or some other agency. During the police action in Mexico, for instance, I was constantly receiving dramatic outlines for war stories and character pieces highlighting our soldiers' bravery. I never spoke with any of the soldiers directly neither to get details nor even confirm said soldier's existence. All I needed for the story was handed to me from the powers that be. Then I flesh it out with whatever details I can find on my own, and if my hunting is fruitless I just make up whatever is missing. If a story is needed to bolster the support of an education cutback, I spin it into an undeniable positive. Statistics, quotes, whatever. I have full freedom and no worries of competition.

I fill a need. I'm young, a minority, and easily

accessible to the next generation.

Something was wrong, however. My chair was adjusted properly, I had turned on my Bartók, but for the first time ever I found myself having serious trouble writing. Seriously. I couldn't write a single sentence. Not one. Everything I wrote was jumbled and came out as mush.

Come on! I met this man! That's got to be worth something. At first I figured I'd just describe him.

Secretary of Christendom Charles Mueller was a man that you could call out to comfortably by first name, despite his holding one of the most prestigious ranks in the world. He was broad-shouldered with speckled hair and the crows-feet around his eyes became more pronounced with age because he frequently smiled in earnest. Speaking simply, he never read from a card or a prompt and his nightly radio casts were his way of aiding our evening prayers and tucking us all in for the night. I grew up listening to his kind, rumbly voice as he assured me and helped me know that God loved me and my nation. And now that man has been assas

I couldn't finish the word. My fingers revolted. Why had Mueller killed himself? It just seemed impossible. He was our father, the voice we pictured God himself to have. He was popular even with other nations. When the Smithsonian was bombed he calmed us, stopped riots with his gentle call to prayer, and eased our paranoia. I tried again.

And now that man has been taken from

I couldn't. I just couldn't. Perhaps my fingers were somehow insisting on writing what they considered the truth? I would indulge them; let them write out whatever crap they wanted, and then afterward produce the article fit to print. I should be done by eight, just in time to call Anne and see how her parents are doing after the ordeal.

I didn't really pay attention as I pounded out whatever my fingers wanted me to say. After about 1,600 words I deleted it and then started on my *actual* article. I spoke of the heinous crime, the wretched atheist Sergent who perpetrated it, and asked for strength and aid in tracking him down. I wrote of how God had blessed our nation, and called our champion Mueller home.

Called him home?

I felt ill, suddenly. A prickly sensation ran through my forearms and hair. Something was really bothering me. I sent off what I had written to Robert. It was good, and filled all needs with the usual flare. The Post would have an excellent front page.

I left the office. I wasn't worried about Robert's feedback because if he didn't like it he'd just call my cell. Besides, it was perfect.

Two subway rides and four blocks later I found myself back on the steps of the National Cathedral. A large group of mourners had formed, preachers preached, flowers were piled and candles lit. Things were in full swing. Civil Seraphim still had an armed presence, but the situation was hardly tense.

I watched them cry, the mourners, and I understood why. I felt the desire to cry too, but years of my profession stunting my emotions kept me at my comfortable distance.

I took the metro away from there and walked around

the lake, all about the cherry blossom trees, wandering from memorial to memorial until night came. Occasionally my phone rang. I looked into Lincoln's stark face; instead of feeling comfort I felt my illness return.

So many locals compare Lincoln's face with that of God. Some confess that his stoney gaze brings them the same ease as being in the Lord's understanding presence.

I looked at those hard eyes, and he looked past me.

Fewer and fewer people were on the streets as I wandered. My phone continued to ring every ten minutes or so. I ignored it. Eventually, while in front of the National Postal Headquarters, I looked at my watch, and saw that it was nearly midnight. Soon the press would be running and my article would be in bold print on the front page. It could be one of the bestselling papers ever. This could solidify and assure my position, even my very name, for generations.

My phone rang again. I was finally enraged with its interruption, so I answered.

"What?!"

"Hung, where the hell are you?" Robert asked on the other end, more curious than worried.

"I've been about. Everything, uh... everything square with the article?" I asked, somewhat relieved it was him calling me and not Anne or her parents or some other person wanting a piece of me.

"Oh sure. Very moving. Your best. I was just calling to congratulate you. Also, Anne's been looking for you. Said you weren't answering your phone so I offered to give it a ring."

"Is she there?"

"In the other room. You guys having problems?"

"No... no..."

"Good. Good." Robert lingered. Something was bugging him. Maybe he couldn't talk over the phone. Usually he didn't try to chat me up like this.

"Want to go for some coffee?" I forced myself to offer. Robert was one of the few people I found myself able to tolerate despite how high strung he was.

"No. I'm good. Thanks though. Say, uh, Hung?" Clearly he had been working up to whatever he was about to ask.

I didn't respond. I just listened to him breathing heavy. Finally he went ahead.

"Hung, I wanted you to know that things have been great working here. I've really enjoyed it. Sometimes… sometimes it feels like we are really doing something important. We seem needed."

I sighed in misery. "We are needed, I suppose."

We were both silent. I figured he might be feeling the same thing I was. Lost. Nearly a century passed before he spoke again.

"Goodnight, Hung."

"Goodnight, Robert."

With that we hung up. I have no idea what he told Anne, but my phone remained silent. I took a cab to my apartment, walked through the door, and slumped on the couch. I wanted to be as close to the door as possible so that when morning came, the paper would be right there.

And it was. I don't even remember falling asleep. Bleary eyed I sprang from the couch and ran to the door, sunshine filling my eyes. The paper sat on my doormat in the hallway, and I snatched it up slamming the front door after me. I unbundled it from its plastic and slapped it out onto the floor, unsure of what I would feel once I read it.

By the first sentence, I saw that this was not the

article written by me, it was the one written by my fingers. My heart sank, and my eyes rose up to the door I had just slammed. I was expecting a knock or perhaps a breach of sorts with CS troops storming in. I rejected the image as soon as it entered my head. If they came, they came. If they didn't, oh well. Maybe I'd just lose my job. Perhaps I'd just disappear from a street corner. I suddenly realized I didn't care, because laid out in front of me in bold print was the truth. Everything The News had said was directly contradicted. Mueller had committed suicide, and the horror of the action was spelled out clear as, well, news in black and white.

I smiled, proud at the trouble I had caused. Curious as to how much I had shaken things up. That's when I noticed that the article had been slightly altered. My fingers had written, in detail, the account of actually witnessing Mueller's death. That part was missing.

The name on the article was Robert Koss. He must have yanked it from my computer when I deleted it somehow, and edited it himself! It isn't uncommon for bosses to have means to spy on their employees. He sent it to print under his name! Only under his influence could it have hit the streets. And there was no mention of me anywhere!

I ran out of the apartment building, and saw my paper in nearly every pair of hands along the store fronts. People were coming up to each other and talking, thumbing through it, and gasping. Confused and worried looks crossed their faces, wrinkling their brows. Somehow, I'm not sure how, but I found myself at the feet of Lincoln. He looked out above me. I tried reading his face, desperate for some hint of Robert's fate.

A fate that could have been mine, if I were a better man.

IV

Lysander Nikodemus

For some, orating is a skill honed through study and practice. Many pursue the ability to speak mellifluously through a multitude of means with aims as broad as the word selection itself, to detail a fact, to validate an opinion, to win an argument, to express passion so that one may rouse it in another...

Or perhaps to sway a mob.

To sway a *mob*.

I say it twice for a reason.

For some orating is a skill, but for me it is a talent. I knew I had it as a child when I was mocked for my ability to speak beyond my years. Mimicking me was a schoolyard game with popularity second to none. As I grew, so did my desire to be heard. New ideas came to me and I had to make them known. Much of the world was wrong, and I had no army, no political staging, no *power* to better it. But God gave me a voice, and in me burned a desire to speak. After all, is that not his greatest gift? His greatest personal power? Did he not *say* 'let there be light?' Was the world not spoken by His voice into existence? He has given us His greatest power and I will not squander it.

So I became a minister of God's word and for the past twenty years I have done my best to emulate His marvelous word with my clumsy human tongue. His graceful diction brought a sky of endless color, while my highfalutin hyperbole gropes to express His will. With divine nomenclature, our Lord God made the sea shimmer green with life, while with meticulously chosen adjectives I can barely fill my pews. My congregation is loyal, but small. Hardly a means to change the world. A world which so needs changing. I always hoped that a single modern individual could change the world and make all the difference. I always, perhaps narcissistically, wished that person to be me.

A young man, weathered far beyond his years, came to me in my office one evening to speak to me privately. He hadn't an appointment, not like he needed one, and the church was almost always empty during the day midweek so I had plenty of time to spare. I had muffins and tea out for him, just in case he was hungry. I am a shepherd, after all.

When I first met this young man it was clear he was troubled. His shoulders rode alongside his ears and the bags under his eyes revealed his lack of rest. With a distracted nod, he took my invitation to sit on my loveseat that I once used for couples' counseling, back when we still actually had couples in the congregation. Ironic that a virgin who had never been in a relationship would give couples counseling. Perhaps that is why I am no longer approached to do it.

After sitting across from me for a minute, pondering if he should sip the tea or not, he finally broke the silence. "I uh... I heard that during the book drives you tend to keep some books to yourself..."

The book drives were often church run and the larger the poundage of collected books the larger the yearly grant from the state. Books that are collected are the usual banned and prohibited fare and mostly paperback with water damage and torn covers. Some churches collect burned books beyond recognition or books that aren't on the list in an effort to pad their federal grants. A church retaining prohibited books from a drive can lead to serious issues, especially certain titles.

"Sir, I don't understand what you mean." I replied coolly.

Reaching into his worn jacket he pulled out a small, leather rectangle with strong binding and sharp corners. Whatever book it was, the quality of its publication and the tenderness of its keeping were obvious. This was a special book.

"I need this book safe, with someone who appreciates it. I heard that you do book drives, but keep the best books. I've heard you even pay for them. But I'm not here for any money or handouts. I just want this book taken care of."

He was direct, and his gaunt stare pierced me like an accuser's would. It was so forceful, yet desperate. Without thinking, my hand extended toward the book. Swallowing hard, he placed it in my grasp. Leaning back in my office chair, I turned it over in my hand, feeling the hollow thump of its weight until its cover faced me.

"Heart of Darkness. Conrad. Banned for being anti-enlightenment." I said. Looking back at him, I saw his eyes were still on the book. "It looks new."

"I've treated the cover a few times, but it hasn't needed much. I've kept it in a plastic bag whenever I wasn't reading it."

I raised a scholarly eyebrow. "What did you think of it?"

"I fucking hated it." He snickered. "It belonged to my brother. So it means a lot though."

I smiled accommodatingly back. "Well, I'll do my best for it."

He nodded solemnly, and then he cried. As he raised his hands to his face I saw that he was missing his left pinkie as well as the tip of his thumb.

We sat in silence once his weeping came to a stop. I had no idea of what to say to such a sudden display of emotional vulnerability, and in hindsight I regret this colossal failure of human stewardship on my part. He just sat there, on my loveseat by himself, and gazed at my rug as though it were some distant paradise he could never reach. After a time, he slipped off his shoes, laid down, and rolled over with his back to me.

Perhaps he had nowhere to go, no place to stay. Maybe he needed to 'crash' from his accumulated stressors. Whatever it was, I placed an afghan blanket over him and let him lie there on my couch in peace.

He slept there silently all afternoon. I eventually left the door unlocked, left him a note and some more muffins in a bag, and walked home to my evening reading and bed.

When I came back in the morning he was gone.

V

Monsignor Michael Joseph Howell III

The Offices of the Honorable Monsignor
Director of Civil Seraphim
Attn. all operatives and assets

My fellow archons and assistant directors,
What we appear to have uncovered here is unprecedented. A one Mr. Robert Koss from The Christendom Post has been uniformly found to be subversive of the state. His article claiming that no assassination had taken place has caused a substantial row, and The Herald and The News are both working damage control. He is now undergoing substantial interrogation in order to ascertain if he is working alone or not and as such The Post's printing has been temporarily suspended and a majority of his staff has been collected for statements. A few staff members have yet to be accounted for however. So investigations are ongoing.
As for the wanted fugitive Albert Sergent, the man-hunt is to be conducted by Archon Wall and his assets. Sergent seems a distinct character, and given Archon Wall's track record he should be in custody sooner rather than later.
Please remember that you are not authorized to give out any information to anyone be they press or family. All releases of information must be released by me, and as such The Herald will report later today on the following:

'The Civil Seraphim is conducting a review of the April 17th assassination of Charles Mueller which occurred on the steps of the National Cathedral. The investigation is in full progress and while in this stage we cannot comment regarding investigative details.
This matter is being taken very seriously. We will uncover the connection between the enemies of the state Robert Koss and Albert Sergent swiftly, and Christ's justice will be delivered upon the United States of Christendom.'

Again, please be vigilant. These are dangerous times, and the people demand justice for their loss. Find Albert Sergent. Find the unaccounted staff members from The Post. Find anyone who is a part of this growing circle of ungodly subversives.

Go with God,
Honorable Monsignor Michael Joseph Howell III
Director
Civil Seraphim

VI

Lysander Nikodemus

The following day was a Thursday, which is typically slow for me, and I looked forward to an indulgent day of reading and micromanagement. The offices of the church were empty and, thinking I was safe, I had just cracked open my favorite book of Blake for some relaxing imagery when I heard a voice.

"That book is banned." The voice observed. Thinking it was the man still residing somewhere hidden in the hallway; I forced a smile without looking up.

"Interesting, coming from-" halfway through my reply I looked up and saw a different man entirely, one dressed in a black suit, black shirt, and a silver tie. His fedora was off, held in his left hand, revealing a shock of blond hair that had streaks of grey before its time. His eyes still looked young, however; an alert neon blue. Standing in my doorway, he waited for me to finish.

"You thought I was someone else." He eventually said. "Who." He held no expression. I knew at once who he was, and the blood in my face was so frightened by his appearance that it fled to my feet for refuge.

"My secretary, Bridget, has a son. He tends to harass me for my reading choices." His face gave no hint of the perception of my lie. "May I help you?"

"My name is Gabriel Wall, with Third Seraph." He held out a silver badge, a cross against a background of six wings radiating from its center. "You had a visitor yesterday. A man named Sergent."

I was shocked. "Sergent? The one in The Paper?" The nation had been abuzz the past few days in regards to a recently uncovered assassination conspiracy involving local atheists and even a few prominent figures including the editor-in-chief of the Christendom Post. If I had given closer attention and taken a greater interest in national doings, I'd probably have known that the wanted man had a deformed hand and would have recognized him at first glance.

Mr. Wall entered my office, looking about. His hands were at his sides as he combed through my room with his eyes, starting at the corner and working his way around to my folding closet door. Behind that door stood a rifle safe that held many books including Sergent's newest addition. It was a locked and secured treasure chest of illegal literature standing within ten feet of the most notorious man from Civil Seraphim.

"The same." He continued. "Tell me about your appointments yesterday. Who came to see you." he said while eying over my mounted photographs one at a time. Most were of fields and trees and rivers, but a few were of the congregation. His eyes settled on one from a bake sale two years ago.

"A young man who didn't leave his name. He came in and we talked for only a moment." I paused, awaiting the next question. Mr. Wall simply kept examining the picture. The silence quickly frightened me, so I filled it. "He spent the night here sleeping on the sofa."

"What were his exact words, Mr. Nikodemus."

"He said that he was homeless and not sure where to turn and only needed a place for one night."

Mr. Wall gave no sign of what he thought of this.

After a few moments of my heavy breathing, he came over to my desk and stood across from me. Reaching down he lifted my book of Blake away from me and read aloud from the top of the current page.

"Tiger, Tiger, burning bright in the forest of the night…" his eyes rapidly scanned back and forth like an old typewriter until he quickly came to the end of the poem. "We just shut down a printing operation of this very poem. Someone producing anti-state pamphlets. We've had a ban on this book for nearly eight years."

"I don't see how this book perpetuates unrest." I gently challenged, trying to sound as innocent as possible.

"It's not *for* you to see." he said, replacing my bookmark properly and handing me back the book. I shivered when my hand brushed against his. "Read what Bridget's son does." He then produced a business card from his breast pocket, expensive and ornate with a silver backing. "If you see him again, discretely call me." With that he walked out. I waited a bit before moving, hoping to hear the distant outside door open and shut, but it never did. Only a shift in the inside air indicated that he had left.

I had heard whispers about Gabriel Wall. Two of my congregation came to me terrified on different occasions, saying that they were afraid for their lives. When they disappeared, rumor had it that the last person to be seen with them was Gabriel Wall. He came to their homes and knocked on their doors, politely holding their coat like an eternal footman. Most lawmen, be they Seraphim or not, prefer to keep out of the public eye. Mr. Wall was the exception. He made his face known, and it immediately put you on the defensive.

If the man I had met really was Sergent, then I pity him. Hated by a nation, hunted by a heartless man in a joyless suit and with no place to go. He wasn't long for this world and despite what he had done I felt somewhat happy that he got a night's rest safely in my office. After all, this is a house of God and I am a shepherd. I offer sanctuary to all who require it, deserving or not.

I turned the book of Blake in my hands, fidgeting with it, and I began to ponder the wisdom of its keeping. A French-cuffed bogeyman had just visited me and he may be back. Oddly enough, he didn't ask me if I knew were Sergent was going. I found it peculiar that one would omit such a question when tracking the most wanted fugitive in the nation.

I stood slowly, trying not to creak my chair, as if Wall were still near, and went to my closet door. Pushing choir robes aside, I turned the knob on it quickly until it thunked open. Inside was my *true* library. Moby Dick (banned for homosexuality), Blake (postulating the intentions of God), Handmaid's Tale (religious slander), and half a burnt book of Nietzsche comprised the crown jewels of my tiny yet growing collection. Moby Dick was in perfect condition and Handmaid's Tale was actually the second printing. I'm particularly proud of those. Resting at the bottom of the rifle safe on an ammo-shelf lay Heart of Darkness, wrapped once again in plastic. I had yet to take the time to incorporate it fully, and in a nervous rush I placed Blake's poetry on top of it.

It wouldn't take much for a man like Mr. Wall to crack open a safe, and then they would all be lost. Suddenly I felt an adrenaline rush of true fear come over me. I envisioned my books burning alight in a pyre, the inked words converted to whisping black smoke, curling up toward the moon as crazed theocrats danced around it singing their hallelujahs.

These books were no longer safe with me. I had to make sure that they were gone before Mr. Wall revisited. To be honest, I had few friends whom I could trust with them. This would take some thinking, and I had to clear my head.

After putting my book back in the safe I changed into shorts and a casual button-up and went outside to the grounds. We had a fabulous garden with mint, onions, and tomatoes for the kitchen. The ingredients were certainly handy for our spaghetti dinners in the reception hall, and occasionally I could round up the congregation children to work the garden with me in the spring. Few things pleased me more than tilling the dirt with my hands, and I could use a little pleasing given my morning visit.

I went to the shed to get my gloves and spade. The lock had rusted into oblivion years before my time here, so I shouldn't have been as surprised as I was to see Sergent in there, asleep like a babe on several stacked bags of peat. Coat rolled up between his knees, he lay on his side silently dreaming, a peaceful look on his face.

I ran inside to my office, tossed papers about until I found Mr. Wall's card, and dialed him. It rang once and then I quickly hung up.

Sergent would be given no right to speak. No chance for proper justice peer judgment. He was doomed, and all I had to do was dial a phone number and his end would come in the form of a starched-collar demon. Sergent deserves to answer to God before answering to the state.

The phone rang in front of me. I backed away from my desk, staring at it as though it would do something fearsome. It rang and rang and rang, echoing louder than I can ever recall, then the answering machine clicked on. Bridget's kind voice chirped a greeting, blessed the caller, and the tone beeped. Silence. No breathing, just a dead yawning silence. I didn't twitch, certain that somehow I was being listened to through my own answering machine.

Eventually, the person on the other line hung-up.

I ran back outside to the shed. I had no plan, no *idea* of what I was going to do. Was I going to keep Mr. Sergent safe within my church? Could he invoke the right to sanctuary? I had no plan, but clearly Sergent did when I opened the shed door. He came out from the shadows, shovel in hand. He swung it over his head in a circle like a berserk Viking and struck me on the shoulder. The blow was feral and swift, glancing upward and striking the side of my head.

VII

Faith Wall

I hate school. And this isn't some 'I hate school because class is boring' or 'I'd rather be painting my nails' kind of hate. This is genuine HATE.

First off, I hate the national prayer at the start of the day. None of the kids care about it, so it comes off as pathetic especially when considering how enthusiastic our principal is when she leads it. Each kid's hand suddenly weighs a metric ton when it has to rise to their heart for the Pledge of Allegiance to the United States of Christendom. And then the mumbling... 'one nation under God blah blah blah blah.'

Secondly, I hate the girls in all my classes. The girls here are catty, judgmental, vain, and conniving. I didn't even know what conniving *meant* in middle school, and now in ninth grade I am learning all *kinds* of things. For instance, girls can chat with you on the phone and be your friend only to get juicy dirt on you and post your texts for all to see on the hallway bulletin board. They will tell you how *great* your cobalt butterfly earrings look and then by the fourth time you wear them, proudly with your hair back, you find out it was all straight-faced sarcasm. If a boy pinches your butt and you do nothing, you're a slut but if you hit him you're a bitch. If you do well in gym you're a butch but if you do badly you're a slag. If you raise your hand too often in class you're trying to sleep with Mr. Vanderbilt but if you sit there and keep to yourself you are emo.

I am learning all kinds of things in school.

The THIRD thing I hate about school is the most obvious and most crushing: my last name. See that cute boy over there? He's smiling at you but WAIT! His buddy just whispered your last name in his ear and now he's too scared to go near you! All those girls that invited you over to their New Year's Eve party only did so because their parents told them to and they want a reason to avoid my father knocking on their door. All my school friends from elementary school and all the kids in the neighborhood I used to play with and ride bikes with are no longer answering my calls or coming to the door because of my father. The higher he climbed in the government the farther everyone got. I can't even babysit anymore!

So, yeah. I *hate* school. I like learning, though. I like science good enough. Biology is pretty cool at times. I like learning about how odd creatures are, and how strange creatures can be like the platypus or fungus. We even learned about fungus that can hijack an ant's body and take it over like an alien and make it climb as high as it can before making it fall to its death. How cool is that?

I'm good at math, but it's boring. There is a kind of pleasure when all your numbers line up and your equation balances just as you thought it would, but I hate my teacher's constant notes demanding I show my work. I mean, who is the teacher here? Me or you?

English is okay. We read mostly essays and detailed accounts of historical events. We also get to study great writers like Laud and Flavius. History is okay, too. We learn about the Bible and Founding Fathers and things like that. We're currently learning about the Corinthians.

I enjoy learning. I do. But I come to school and set aside all of this hate for one reason... art. My art teacher is an older lady named Clementine and she *clearly* had too much fun in her younger years. Faded tattoos and yellowed teeth say as much. We always get to listen to classical music and despite being told what medium to use, we can usually paint/sculpt/draw/sketch what we are feeling. I love this because I have yet to meet anyone who is as good at drawing as I am, and nobody dares make fun of me for it. It's my safe place.

Back-to-school night is coming up soon, and Clementine asked us yesterday to all paint a portrait of God for the hallways. We have been given free use of any of the art materials and we have a whole week to make it. Margret Jones is using pastels, but she can't shade very well and her Jesus looks like he has a skin condition. Trenton Myers is making a paper-cut out of God; white cotton-balls for a beard. Valery is making a Russian Icon of sorts with a man-Jesus in Mary's arms looking all creepy and whatnot. Ben is just painting the American flag.

Everyone is making God and Jesus and Mary all looking perfectly white and handsome and all physically fit. But what if Jesus were a fatty? I don't mean for anyone to think I'm trying to go to Hell or anything, but would people have said 'he is our savior!' if he had a 50 inch waist? How many Romans would it take to hoist the fat-ass Lamb of God onto the cross? Would they need an extra-large cross? Would more people have come up to Golgotha to watch for kicks? To see the tubby savior jiggle in pain while he cried out 'it is finished?'

I didn't say any of this out loud, but man I wanted to. Clementine would probably try to constructively redirect me, but it would fuel the drama-fire in school for months. I'm curious to see if they would even *dare* try and call my father in for a teacher-parent conference.

And that is when I knew what to do. I was going to paint a fat Jesus on the cross. He'll have teeth missing and kinky hair like a Mexican. He'll have saggy man-boobs and I'll make his ankles chubby like the lady who works in the principal's office.

That's it! I will paint the worst Jesus anyone has ever seen. No more rippling-stomached savior of man! This Jesus will be uncomfortable to look at. And *I* will make them look at him.

VIII

Albert Sergent

We live in a world of lies. Obvious ones, at that. I am not the only one to see them, but I wish I wasn't the only one that got angry with them.

I must stay focused. I currently have a poor reverend tied up unconscious on his couch with an icepack on his head, and according to the flyer on his desk he has service TONIGHT. I've already gone through his pockets and snagged his credit card and house keys, but I have no idea where his car keys are. Even if I had them, I'm not sure how much good a car will do me. I've seen the road blocks and this city is crawling with cops, Civil Seraph, and all kinds of citizens who couldn't wait to see me strung up.

Counter-intuitive as it is, taking the Metro or the road is a bad move. Hanging tight for a bit and maybe nabbing a bicycle or something might be the only thing that can give me a chance. I should still find the car keys just in case, so I can jump in, drive hard, and dump it if I need to.

As for money, I can only use this credit card once and locally, because if I use it while moving it will plot my course like dots on a graph. I'm not doing that.

I could really use a gun. A gun would be nice. I doubt Nik here has one. Actually, a gun would be dumb. Nevermind. It would simply raise attention if I am questioned, and if I have to fire it I've already been had anyways.

It would be nice to hold one, though. The illusion of power would be welcome, despite being unreal.

Good. Nik's got a big ol' bump on his noggin, which means his bruising is external and he'll likely be fine. Heh. He's a lightweight and it didn't take much to knock him out. In another minute or two I'll make sure he is sitting up and awake. I don't want to hit the ten minute mark of him being out after a head injury. That is *really* bad for you.

I wish Sean was here. I wish the voice I hear in my head when I think was his.

IX

Lysander Nikodemus

He must have dragged me to the couch in the office. I came to, my wrists and ankles bound with lamp cord. He was over at Bridget's desk, breaking the lock on her pen drawer. With three hard hits of a letter opener, he popped it open. He was collecting her loose change. Looking about, I saw that he had already thrown my coat to the floor after looting it of what little cash I carried.

"You're not going to get far with that little money." I said, the sound of my voice making my head ache. There was a terrible pain behind my eyes, throbbing and contracting.

He looked to me, like a bird realizing it was being stalked.

"I'm not going to get far, money or not." He replied, rolling the quarters into paper slips that Bridget kept for the bank deposits. "I know your head hurts. Can you see?" he asked.

"Well enough." I replied tersely.

He put a roll of quarters in each pocket and left the rest of the change. Moving with purpose, he strode over to me and rolled me onto my side. I recoiled at first, and in response he himself flinched.

"Close one eye. Close it." He gently commanded. I did.

"Now can you see fine out of it?"

"Yes, I think so."

"Good, now the other."

I did as he said. "I can see fine out of that one too." I told him. It was like I was getting an eye exam, Sergent craning over me with one hand hoisting my head.

"You still have a concussion, so you need to keep off your feet." he diagnosed. I snorted at him.

"It's a good thing that you tied me up then. Clearly you don't want me hurting myself. You know, I wasn't going to turn you in. I wasn't going to call anybody."

Sergent didn't say anything as he started dumping out drawers and tipping over things. He was looking for something.

"When is your assistant due in?" he asked in a huff.

"Bridget comes in around five to get things ready for evening service. It's just she and I tonight. People will notice when the altar is empty."

At this Sergent yanked the phone from the desk and brought it over to me. "You're going to call her and tell her not to come tonight."

"I'm not calling anyone." I snapped, without thinking.

"You're calling Bridget because you don't want her walking into this situation and escalating it. Let's keep her out of harm's way." he persisted. "Where's her number?"

"I was just on the phone with her. You can redial it."

"To hell with that." He said, setting the phone down and locating the Rolodex. Thumbing through it, he found her number quickly. He dialed, and held the receiver up to my ear. "Your excuse had better be believable. No codes. I'm right here watching."

It rang five times and went to her machine. I swallowed hard and began.

"Hi Bridget. Nancy just gave a ring and said she'd

come by and help tonight. So, take the night off and enjoy yourself. And make it an early night because I actually need you in at around six in the morning tomorrow. I have a contractor coming by for that leak and that was the only time I could book him. Goodnight. See you tomorrow."

Sergent hung up the phone.

"Good. Saved your life just then, assuming that there's actually a leak and someone named Nancy."

After hearing his threat, I had to ask. "Did you really kill Mueller?"

Halfway to putting the phone back, he froze. Slowly turning, his eyes first looked right into mine, and then they trailed off to somewhere more puzzling.

"Of course I did." He said flatly, setting the phone down. Putting his misshapen hand to his face, he rubbed his eyes as though waking himself from a fog.

"Are you going to kill me too?" I asked, oddly being detached from the fear for my life.

"Not if you behave. Tonight you're going to give your service and no one will know anything. I'll be gone soon after, so long as you tell me where your car keys are."

I spent the rest of the afternoon on the couch. He kept me bound, but flipped me over onto my back, feet up on a pillow and a bag of ice balanced onto the side of my head.

"How's your head?" he asked. I just offered that it hurt. "You were hit with a shovel, you know." He smiled.

Around three o'clock he walked out of the room. He just up and left. My mind went frantic! The possibility of escape came to me and I began strategizing how I should roll to my feet, which door I should hop to, who I should call out for once outside. I was screwing my courage to the sticking place when he came back in. He had only been gone for a minute. In his hand was a wrapped loaf of cranberry nut bread on top of a plate that he had found in the kitchen fridge. Looking about, he grabbed the letter opener. Then he dragged a chair up next to me.

"Sit up a bit." he said. I wiggled up to my elbows. Peeling open the bread, he began clumsily slicing it. "No biting. This is my good hand." he said as he brought a bit of loaf to my mouth.

"How did that happen? To your hand?" I asked, looking at the food reluctantly.

"Eat and I'll tell you."

So I ate, and as he fed me slowly, he sighed. "I grew up in the projects, or what used to be the projects so my neighborhood was rough. The other kids weren't too keen on me, me being atheist and all. They figured they could get me to call out for God's help if they held me down and tortured me a bit. Tore up my palm, snipped my fingers, and they used matches too. I never called out to God, though. Not out of stubbornness or anything, it just didn't really seem to be what would save me. It never did."

"Why don't you believe in God, Sergent?"

"I just never believed. I don't know, I just didn't. I didn't feel it there. This 'presence' everyone speaks about just never was in me, I guess."

I didn't know what to say. So often I had practiced in front of the mirror how I would convert someone, to bring them into God's healing light. Here was my chance: my opportunity to talk this man into the Lord's grace, to set down his letter opener, unbind me, and turn himself in without incident.

Yet I said nothing, looking at that hand of his and seeing him eye over the cranberry bread with personal, hungry need. He had fed me first, I realized.

About an hour before service he hoisted me to my feet, which made me incredibly dizzy, and tied me against the heater under the window. "There are two barrels of gasoline in the shed. I will use them to burn your church to the ground if anything happens. I will be listening."

He was in and out of the office a lot after that. He brought several drums of fuel in, took the tops off, and let the fumes fill the air. With a couple of quick jolts of one of the cans, he splashed fuel onto the walls. "This is only half of it. The rest I poured in various places. I'm going to untie you, let you use the bathroom after I scout it out, and you're going to get dressed. I will be with you."

And he was. Preparing the wine, sacrament, and everything. He was shadowing me; at my heels the entire time.

"I usually greet the congregation as it filters in." I told him, once dressed in my vestment.

"Not today." was his reply. Several people came in through the main door, regulars, and they found their usual seats. Sergent eyed them over through the cracked office door. He turned to me and snarled, feral once again. "You can whisper for help, shout even, but no one will be able to stop me from setting the blaze. Starting with your office."

My books. All I could think of was my books. Everyone would be able to get out in time and burning the church down, though be it God's house, would accomplish nothing. But burn the books...

"Your book is in there." I said, finally feeling some level of leverage. "But you'll have no trouble from me."

He gave me a long, evaluating look. "Fair enough." he conceded.

Time came, and I walked out to my podium. With the kerosene out of my nose, it was easier to focus. There were about twelve people there, which was a surprisingly good gathering for a Thursday. Mrs. Tanner sat right up front; done up as usual with her sculpted blue hair and tilted hat. The quiet Mrs. McPhearson was also present. She was particularly impossible to miss, given that she was an extraordinary Latin beauty. There were others, some with somber expressions from the lingering memory of Mueller's assassination, the cause of their loss just behind me and to the right peeking through a cracked door.

I began to think of it, my head still aching. For a moment I considered calling out for aid, chancing that Sergent would only run instead of taking the time to destroy what he could, especially his Heart of Darkness.

And then I spied Mr. Wall, sitting erect like a soldier in the left section. No one sat near him. Against his dark suit and the green pews his cold steel eyes blazed like hot blue stars. It terrified me.

"Today…" I started, winging it for I had had no time to prepare. "I would like to speak of redemption. I would like to emphasize the need for it, what it does for us once we've given it to ourselves, and what happens to the psyche when one is denied the right to redeem themselves to the world, their loved ones, and Christ. Forgiveness is the acknowledgment of wrong, and loving those that wronged you. Redemption, however… redemption is how the wrong can be made right."

No passages were read. It was nothing but my impassioned speaking, about our right to God's love. Time quickly passed, and looking back I can't remember what I said. The sacrament was offered by me alone and not long after everyone stood to leave. I bid them all goodnight. Mrs. Tanner came up to me, grabbed my forearm, and shook it about with enthusiasm.

"That's what I like! When you let loose!" she smiled. I reminded her that we needed her muffins for this coming Sunday, and it pleased her so. Surprisingly Mrs. McPhearson came up to me, and as soon as Mrs. Tanner was out of ear-shot, she spoke.

"The man in the suit. Do you know why he is here?" It was too easy to watch her lips when she spoke.

"Oh, he's here to meet with me after service."

She nodded, but hesitated before following Mrs. Tanner out. "It was a wonderful service this evening."

Eventually everyone left, save Mr. Wall, and their footsteps could no longer be heard outside on the walkway. I felt horribly guilty for not standing by the door to shake all of their hands, especially with such a large crowd on such a well-received night.

As steadily as I could, I walked down the side stairs that flanked the altar and made my way to Mr. Wall, who still sat calmly in his pew flipping through a bible.

"What did you do to your head." he asked while thumbing through Exodus. He must have spotted the swelling bruise through my hair. Or noticed my walk somehow? My fear began to rebuild.

"A paint can slipped from a shelf in the shed. Bonked my head pretty well."

He didn't say anything. Time passed, me standing at his side, him seemingly ignoring me.

"Is there anything I can do for you Mr. Wall?" I asked with a tremble in my voice. I suddenly was sure that I had blown it.

He snapped the bible shut, and rose to his feet. "I wanted to leave my card with Bridget. But I haven't seen her."

"Ah, yes. She's at home. Took the night off." I

reached out my hand to him. "But I can see that she gets it."

"I'm going to leave it on her desk, I think." And with that he stood, walking toward the back door. I froze, searching and grasping for something clever to save Sergent, or Mr. Wall as the case may be. I'm not a clever man, however, but a reverent one.

"Do not shed blood in His house!" I commanded him, my voice so stern and willful that it surprised even me.

He stopped dead in his tracks with his back to me, and neither of us moved for a time.

Reaching into his coat, he drew his gun. Slowly his eyes scanned about and settled on the door I had walked out from prior to service. Stalking toward it, moving past it, keeping his weapon low, he crept. I was helpless. I couldn't think of anything to say or do, my hands empty at my side, my feet fixed to the floor. All I normally had were words, and they had fled me.

He placed an ear against the wall. Reaching into his inner jacket pocket, Mr. Wall produced a small box-shaped object. I've prided myself in not knowing much about weapons, but I could recognize from the ring on the side that this was a grenade of some kind.

"No!" I screamed, running right at him, fearful that any explosion or flame could set off the kerosene cans within the office. He raised his gun at me, and at the same time Sergent jumped out, fist in full swing, and he hammered Mr. Wall right in the face. The weapon went off, firing in some random tangent, the flame from the gun made enormous from the fumes of the open cans. Both men were immediately on fire. Sergent ran in full sprint, smoke, flames and all, right down the aisle and Mr. Wall rolled around frantically to put out his flames without so much as a yelp. Gunfire erupted outside and I ran to see. If Albert was shot, hurting, or dying, he had the right to a man of the cloth.

"You go *nowhere*, Nikodemus!" Mr. Wall roared from far behind me. I turned to see him lurching to his feet; pistol trained to me, with smoke rising from the shoulders of his jacket as though his anger were made visible.

X

Rosa McPhearson

You know you hate your life when your best comfort comes from daydreaming about your childhood. I close my eyes and I'm eight again, picking berries with my sister by Santa Concorsa River. It's summer, and the neighbor's boy shyly brings me flowers, running away as soon as the stems are in my hand...

Then I wake next to my snoring husband, who's rolled on his side facing me with his eyes tightly shut. I can see the stress in his face even while he sleeps, his crow's feet deepened by the predawn shadows. I brush his bangs from his forehead so I can see his face better. Teddy is an idealist, and still the handsome man I fell in love with.

I often wander the house in the middle of the night, checking the locks and windows, and looking in on the boys. I'm up at least two times every night, and it's part of my routine.

Morning comes, and I've got breakfast on the table as everyone walks in bleary-eyed. The boys get a kiss on the forehead each, and Ted gets one on the cheek. Lunches are deployed, backpacks are mounted, and Ted checks his tie in the hall mirror one last time. People make jokes and off color remarks about lawyers, claiming them to be the lowest of life. That kind of rhetoric has always been lost on me, because Teddy's the only lawyer I've ever known.

Away they go in the van, with me standing in the

doorway as always, waving goodbye in my bathrobe. The younger of my two sons, Finny, always makes a point of waving goodbye until I'm out of sight. He's a gentle boy, not as rambunctious as his older brother John. Finny doesn't look much like Teddy, his face gaunter and his eyes a bit more narrow with a hint of sadness. He always asks me how my day was.

May he never know.

The next part of my morning routine is the ferocious, tedious, blazingly fast process of make-up, jewelry, stockings, shoes, and worst of all 'hair' that can only be accomplished when the house is empty. My hair is a thick, unwieldy beast that must be tamed every single morning.

I'm out the door, in the car, and stuck in cutthroat traffic on the capital beltway within the hour. After the vehicular battle that is my a.m. commute, I arrive at the Department of Civil Seraphim. My parking spot is the second best in the garage. On my way in, everyone bids me good morning in various ways ranging from professional to leering.

"Good morning, Mrs. McPhearson." Gabriel Wall says as he passes. Word has it in the lunchroom that I'm the only one he ever greets. There are many popular, not to mention lurid, theories as to why.

Today, however, I try to catch him as he goes by. He sees me open my mouth to speak as I turn to follow him.

"I'll come by after seeing the Monsignor." he calls over his shoulder, a stack of books under his arm as he storms his way up some stairs and disappears amongst the crowd.

Before entering Monsignor Howell's office, the moment everyday when my fingers grip the long brass handle to his glass double doors, I try not to hate the world.

I swallow hard, and enter.

The waiting area is all marble, with potted trees, leather chairs, and glass coffee tables. My desk is enormous and of the finest English oak. I put my purse in the lowest drawer on the left and start checking my email. The door to the Monsignor's personal office is behind me to my left, and his conference room door is to my right. He's already in, thank God. And from the sounds of it through the wall, so is Gabriel. Gabriel's voice is so low that it can't be heard, so whenever they have their one on one meetings it sounds like the Monsignor is talking to himself. It ends quickly, the door opens, and Gabriel walks out. He comes up to my desk, his arms hanging in front of him with his hands folded.

"Your preacher is in a bit of trouble. Seen The News?" he asked. He wasn't being curt either, just forthright.

"I saw your men get out of the car and shoot at Sergent as he ran away." Gabriel, as of late, has been traveling with three other men. The Monsignor wants more Seraphim like Gabriel, apparently, and figures that by shadowing and assisting him they'll be just as well trained and loyal.

"They aren't my men." he responded flatly. Gabriel made it known, in his own subtle way that he hated the idea.

"I've been attending Nikodemus' weeknight sermons for three years now and he has never struck me as a man of violence. He preaches peace."

"I heard. But the matter remains that he continued to hide Sergent from me when I gave him every opportunity.

- 54 -

The courts will decide his level of involvement. And he had a contraband cache."

"Is there any way I can testify on behalf of his character?"

"Of course. I'll email you a form to print out and fill in. Just get it in my inbox and I'll make sure it goes where it needs to." he said, looking me in the eye as always. Most men look about or examine me unsettlingly when speaking to me. But Gabriel always looks me dead in the eye, never flinching. I do the same to him. It takes effort, especially during his infamous long silences. "Is there anything else you needed?" he asked.

"No, I was just worried for him. Also, didn't you get burned?" I ask, suddenly remembering.

He looked about to see that the Monsignor was nowhere within earshot. "Yes." he finally admitted. "Along the right arm and shoulder. I've got some cream and bandages on."

"You look like nothing happened." I mildly complimented.

"That is always the point." he nodded, closing his eyes briefly to gesture a 'thank you.'

"Rosa, dear, could you come in here with some coffee?" Howell called in his aged smoker's voice. "We've got to make some changes with today's schedule. It might take a while."

Gabriel's gaze did not leave me. I gathered up several folders, a binder, and my organizer and stood. Odd as it sounds, I was leaving Gabriel's safety and I could feel those bright, baby eyes of his on the back of my head as I went in.

"Shut the door behind you, if you please Rosa." Howell requested.

You don't need to know the rest.

I don't know how it started. Somehow I forgot. But I never found the Monsignor attractive and I never have entertained thoughts of straying from my husband. This thing, this 'relationship' is one sided and I am trapped. I couldn't say 'no' because it was overtly implied that my husband's career and my children's futures were at stake. Trying to shake Howell's interest, I began dressing more conservatively, wearing less and less make-up, and buying shoes with no heel. He said something along the lines of 'your appearance represents me. You should be at your best.'

Neither of my sons has ever had a birthday where their mother had not, earlier that day been... I don't even know the word for it. What it is that the respectable Monsignor Michael Howell and I do.

And I can't even bring myself to describe what he looks like. I'm sure however you visualize him will be just fine.

When I get home, I have the strength to hug and kiss my husband, be excited about John's afternoon sports, and hear all about the amazing things Finny learned in math class. But when Finny asks me how my day was, a small part of me wants to tell him. Wants to tell someone who'll care. One time I must have woken him in the middle of the night while I was crying on the couch downstairs. He didn't ask what was wrong. Not a word came out of his mouth. He just held me. Held mommy.

After we were done, the Monsignor and I, he gave me the objectives of the day. I jotted them down hastily while getting dressed.

"First things first, Sergent is still out there. I want people connected; unified on the local level to find him. I want them walking through the woods holding hands like they were searching for a lost child. He needs to be found by an everyman. His tangle with Gabriel makes *great* news, but I want a 'nobody' to become a national hero by getting their photo taken and getting interviews on The News. Give the Secretary of State a call, as well as the Vice President's assistant . . . whatever his name is, and tell them both to get something organized through the local precincts."

About then I discovered my watch on the floor. The band had broken and it must have come off during. For years Teddy has just thought me careless, losing earrings and breaking necklaces. Bruises on my legs are often explained by me bumping into something like a waste can or desk corner. He affectionately calls me klutzy, and uses it as an excuse to take me shopping for jewelry. Finally being a partner, he can afford to dote over me and few things give him more pleasure.

I'm glad he's not more perceptive.

"Also!" the Monsignor continued. "This Nikodemus fellow is perfect. He fits the description of a miscreant. He preaches counter culture and pacifism and harbors dangerous texts. I want his congregation subtly demonized and the church itself closed down as a crime zone. Scandals are to gradually unveil, revealing a plot between Sergent, Koss, and Nikodemus. I want the assassination of Mueller to be the tip of the iceberg, and their nefarious plots to be foiled by our very own Civil Seraphim with the help of the common man."

He didn't know that I was there last night, at Nikodemus' service? The Monsignor, as usual, just didn't read the report. Or perhaps Gabriel omitted me...

"Don't worry about calling the White House. I'm

going by there today. And, on second thought, don't bother calling the Secretary. He and I will talk. Also, send more flowers to Mueller's family. Make them nice." He seemed to suddenly remember where he was, and he turned to watch me furiously scribbling. "How're your two boys doing, Rosa?" He usually asks these kinds of questions afterward. I'm not sure if he's threatening me or just trying to make me run off to the ladies room to cry. Maybe he feels empowered, knowing me to be married and committed to a family.

I mumble a traditional response, pretending to be focused in my scribbling.

"And that youngest boy of yours, Finny. How is he? Healthy?"

I felt my arms electrify with goose bumps and my face prickle from my body temperature suddenly growing hot. He'd never mentioned my son's name before. He'd never spoken of either of them directly like that.

I was at a loss. "He's fine. Fine and well. Thank you." I almost spoke of how impressive his math skills were, because that's how I normally gush about him, but the Monsignor didn't deserve to know such things about someone so special.

He nodded, smiled, and sat down in his chair. Turning his back to me he spoke out. "Let's get the day going. I've got that lunch so I won't be seeing you a lot today."

I brushed myself up in the ladies room as discreetly as possible. It's hard getting away with it nearly every morning without being noticed. My guess is that my ritual is potent fuel for the rumor regarding my supposed affair with Gabriel.

When I got back to my desk, Gabriel had emailed

me the paperwork he promised. Despite my priorities, I printed it out and took care of it first. I filled everything in and spent half an hour writing, in as much factual and emotionally removed detail as possible, about how good a man Nikodemus was. After I had dropped it into Gabriel's inbox, I went about my phone calls. Faxes were sent and signatures were requested. Meetings were canceled and rescheduled. Promises were made third hand, and soon broken. It was what I did.

Usually I could just get to it, grinding away at my daily checklist while running from office to office with paperwork and demands. Today, though, I just kept making mistakes. I called people by the wrong name and delivered the wrong forms as well as dialed the wrong phone numbers. The image of him, *him*, asking about Finny would not leave my mind.

XI

Gabriel Wall

Auto transcript of audio file TRN112839043
Sub Operation: Mueller Assassination
Subject interviewed: Mr. Lysander Aaron Nikodemus
07:20 am ███████████████
Interviewer: Archon Gabriel Wall

GW: Good morning. I know you have not slept, but
this will be your final interview for now and
then you will be submitted to containment
for non-violent offenders. Everything you
say is an official statement. I will be asking
you questions about you, your associates,
Albert Sergent, and your doings.

pause

GW: Alright, so let's start with the obvious
question: why did you house and aid a
wanted person of high profile?

LAN: We both know he had taken me hostage. I
have the injury to prove it, and I bet you
could find the lamp cord used to tie me up.

Oh, and I didn't just wreck my own office.

GW: So you are saying you did not house or aid this man willingly?

LAN: No.

GW: Where did you initially find him on the day that you were held hostage?

LAN: In our shed, out back.

GW: What was he doing there?

LAN: Sleeping.

GW: And from a sleeping position he struck you on the head with a three foot long shovel?

LAN: No, I—I went inside to call you.

GW: You did. And I called back and got only a voicemail machine.

LAN: I didn't want you to kill him.

GW: I had no intention of—

LAN: You had a grenade.

GW: A flashbang. A flashbang temporarily blinds and disorients the target for easy and safer apprehension. I would have taken him into custody without any injury, yet as it is Mr. Sergent is currently on the run with a bullet wound and in dire need of medical attention.

LAN: You also had your gun out!

GW: I only use my sidearm when it is absolutely
the last resort. I want Mr. Sergent alive so
he can be tried by a jury of his peers.

LAN: Earlier you said he was an atheist. If so, his
peers can't serve on a jury.

GW: We are getting sidetracked. Now, I answered
some of your concerns about my actions.
Let's return to some of yours. Mr. Sergent
had the keys to your car and used it briefly
to move several blocks away. Did you give
him these keys?

LAN: I told him where they were, eventually. Yes.

GW: Does he have the keys to any other vehicles,
sheds, storage units, or homes aside from
yours?

LAN: Not that I know of.

GW: Did you tell him where to go to hide?

LAN: No.

GW: Did you offer any advice whatsoever?

LAN: No. Wait, well, yes. He was looking for
loose change in my desk and I told him he
wouldn't get far on it.

GW: Did you advise him to take a roll of quarters?

LAN: Um, no. Why?

GW: He used the roll of quarters as a weapon on me. Where did he say he was going after tonight?

LAN: He didn't say.

GW: What were his plans after tonight?

LAN: He didn't say.

GW: Who did he plot with?

LAN: He said nothing about that.

GW: Did he speak about Secretary Charles Mueller's murder in detail?

LAN: No.

Audible sigh

GW: Did he speak about Mueller's murder at all?

LAN: I asked him if he had killed him, and he said yes.

GW: Alright. Let's change the subject for a bit. Tell me about the vault of books in your office that are all prohibited by the 32nd Amendment.

pause

LAN: They are books.

GW: Indeed. And how long did it take to build your
    collection in that vault?

LAN: I don't really know. I just would come across
    them and hang onto to them.

GW: Why?

LAN: They are literature. Great works. People
    made them.

GW: So you are preserving art?

LAN: Yes.

GW: The Library of Congress has all of these
    books preserved.

LAN: I know.

GW: So why would you not turn them in?

LAN: Because people aren't allowed to read them.

GW: Is that the same logic behind your shelves of
    books at home?

    pause

LAN: Yes.

GW: They are prominently displayed. Do you
    invite people over to view them?

LAN: No.

GW: Do people borrow them from you?

LAN: No.

GW: Who have you lent books out to?

LAN: Nobody.

GW: Bridget says that her son borrows them time to time.

LAN: The young man is at college. How could he?

GW: We have him in custody and he is being transferred to DC.

LAN: Wait, what? Why!? They are my books!

GW: Bridget is also in custody as we investigate your congregation and church.

LAN: I don't understand!

GW: Does your church have any unsanctioned meetings, clubs, or events?

LAN: Why would you arrest Bridget?

GW: She hasn't been charged with anything as of yet. Does your church have any unsanctioned meetings, clubs, or events?

LAN: No! We do bake sales, bingo, and a small singing group! Can we sing!? Are we allowed to sing?!

GW: What do you sing?

LAN: Hymns!

GW: There is no problem with that. Do you know

where Albert Sergent might be?

LAN: No!

GW: Did you meet him prior to yesterday?

LAN: You know I did. I already told you when we
first met! He came by the office!

GW: To do what?

pause

LAN: Deliver one of the marvelous books you fear
so much.

GW: And how did he know that you would take it?

silence

GW: How did he know you kept books?

silence

GW: How many people are in your book network?

silence

GW: How many of these books has Albert Sergent
read?

silence

XII

Lysander Nikodemus

I was as methodical and detailed as I could be when I explained to the intake officer my reasons for frustration. Despite being exhausted from talking, especially to Wall, I made it clear that I was to be transferred to a different wing of the prison, one where non-violent offenders were kept since I was neither a thug nor a thief.

Yet here I was, sitting in the intake room for the violent offenders. The officer opposite me nodded thoughtfully, head bowed and eyes up gazing at me over the rims of his glasses; his folded hands drummed their fingers on his round belly.

"Monsignor Howell made it *real* clear to us which wing you would be in here at the DC." He muttered with a lazy exhalation. Standing up and opening the door for me, he led me out and down the hallway. The jumpsuit I wore was a bit too loose, but it was crisp and starched and despite my shoes having been worn by many previous detainees, they were comfortable enough.

I wondered if they would have books here, or a library. Maybe I can spend my days waiting in a chair somewhere reading until the trial is sorted out, and Gabriel realizes his error.

Several barriers of steel metal bars slid open by way of invisible hands as we got closer to a riveted door. It swung open slowly as if it contained a vault of precious treasure beyond.

"Hey, listen up everyone!" he barked as soon as he entered. Each vibrant jumpsuit within my vision over his shoulder halted and each pair of eyes first found him, and soon after me. "This here is a *preacherman* who is a part of a violent organization, but he is under the impression that he shouldn't be in our wing because he thinks he himself ain't violent! Be certain to treat him properly and with respect! Remember, he is *not* a violent man!"

With a hostile and dismissive slap on my back, he stepped out and the door clanged behind me.

The ceiling was high, the walls concrete, and the collective gaze of the room's population pierced me. My first impression was that they were judgmental men and each had swiftly evaluated me and found me lacking. Whatever had held their attention prior to their interruption quickly drew them back, however, and they continued to drift about their prison routine of cards, chess, lounging, and reading.

"I'm Cray. I'm the *guy* around here." A deep, rich voice rumbled down my neck from behind me. How he got there without my seeing is beyond me. Turning I saw that Cray was a large man, terrifying and yet charismatic in his presentation. His smile disarmed me, and his tattoos told the storied tale of Christ's end as a mortal.

Each muscle was an oiled, polished surface dedicated to a station of Christ's suffering on the cross. His neon orange jumpsuit was rolled down to his waist prominently displaying the murals of his devotion. Behind him, on either side, stood two smaller yet no less intimidating men. One of them had tears tattooed to the corners of his eyes and the other had his eyebrows and ears notched decoratively.

Cray and his entourage stood proudly before me, Christ's visage in agony all over his chest, and he beamed.

"Fellow man of Christ, eh?" he smiled.

I nodded conservatively.

"Is hard here, being a man of the word. Is hard here all the time. We just waiting to be moved around, so there's no time to make prayer groups."

"I could lead one, if you like." I chanced.

This was clearly what Cray was hoping for. With a meaty hand on my shoulder he cooed. "That be perfect, son. Perfect! I'm on pod three, third door. Boys will let you in, son. Tonight? After chow around seven?"

Shyly, I nodded. I wouldn't dare be late.

As the afternoon rolled on I studied the bible provided to me intensely, noting the differences in this federal translation when compared to those of my King James. Often the word 'glory' was replaced with 'power' and Christ himself was paraphrased during the last supper in a truncated manner. I couldn't discern the reason, but the washing of his disciples feet didn't have the tender resonance that I was accustomed to.

Dinner time came. I sat in the first empty place I could find, my rear nearly half off of the seat in an effort to give the elbow next to me all the space it could wish for. Luckily, the man sitting beside me had the same idea, and scarfed his food with the same scared and frantic manner as I did. Loquaciousness did not seem to be a viable character trait your first day in a maximum security jail.

I ate quickly, put my tray away, and kept movements minimal in order to blend in as best I could without drawing the ire of judging eyes.

I followed the arrows to pod three, God's book in hand as if to protect me. I was reciting in my mind a graceful means to introduce myself more formally when I bumped into the man with the tears.

"Hey." He grunted. "We meeting down here. More room. More people." He motion for me to follow him. It was a good opportunity to see the working guts of the building including laundry facilities and what looked like a room for book storage and board games.

My gut rose up against my heart, causing its heavy beat to jar my whole body with each thump. My ears burned red and their heat was almost painful, convincing me that they were luminescent.

My guide brought me into what looked like a small hallway with different meeting rooms behind thick doors. One was ajar, splashing light into an otherwise dim space.

We went in. The room itself was comfortable and almost like an apartment. There was a weathered couch, two battered yet warm looking lounge chairs, and hotel art on the walls. The wooden paneling on the walls was clearly outdated in both decorative fashion and luster, but it meant that the room had been built for its occupants to feel normal.

It reminded me of my common room in seminary, and thusly my heart eased.

"Holy Roller!" Cray declared as I entered. He moved making a space for me on the couch next to him. "Come 'n and sit down, son!" He patted the vacant cushion next to his paw.

The third man from before was kicked back in one of the lounge chairs, bible in hand, thumbing casually. He didn't acknowledge my existence, and was perhaps selecting a passage of relevance for the evening.

A little anxious, I sat on the couch next to Cray. He flopped his arm over my shoulders and clenched me for a moment in greeting, his thick arm feeling as strong as a workhorse's leg. The man who guided me in, infinitely weeping man, sat on my other side. I suspected that this couch wasn't built with the intention of comfortably resting three men, even if one of them was smallish like myself.

Cray pondered for a moment, eyeing me over with anticipation of the evening's reading. "You a holy man, right? That's what I heard. You holy."

"No more than any other man, really."

"A preacher? Got your own church, right?"

"Right. It's lovely." A pang wretched my soul, and I envisioned my poor church being torn down, or worse yet seized and repurposed to some other congregation. Would they still have a job for Bridget? Would the new priest be to Mrs. Tanner's liking?

"Well..." Cray said in thought, but something told me he had already arrived at whatever decision he was going to make long ago. "How bout something from Luke six? We like us some Luke."

"All about Luke around here." The man in the chair chimed in passively.

I flipped my bible open, quickly found the page despite unsteady hands, and landed on verse 27. Clearing my throat and projecting my voice as if at the pulpit, I began.

"But to you who are listening, I say this: Love your enemies, do good to those who hate you, bless those who curse you, pray for those who mistreat you. If someone slaps you on one cheek, turn to them the other also." The infinite crier stood up from the couch, and walked to the door closing it. "If someone takes your coat, do not withhold your shirt from them."

He walked back over to the couch and punched me so hard in the face I saw white. It was a lightning fast strike, brutal and sudden, and my head banged into Cray's chest as a result.

Cray's hands snapped onto my shoulders, and held me like a misbehaving child.

"Why you stop reading?! I need to hear the word! Keep reading!" He snarled, the smile and impish charm evaporated.

I coughed. My lips felt blood from my nose.

"I-I don't understand."

"READ!" Cray roared.

I cleared my throat, this time in necessity instead of in habit, and continued. "Give to everyone who asks, and if anyone takes what belongs to you, do not demand…" my nose was dripping blood onto the page, soaking through the thin sheets. I was desperate to wipe it off when I was hit again.

More white.

"Keep reading the good word!" Cray snapped as he pulled the bible from my hands. He slapped me like I suspect he would a woman. The other two men were upon me now, tearing off my shoes and shoving me face down onto the couch. "Get him up on his knees. Yeah. Like that." He casually ordered them.

With my head down, my bottom in the air, and shoes off, he placed the open bible under my face. "You keep on reading, Holy Roller." He cooed with evil glee. "You don't bleed none on this couch. You keep reading while we fuck you."

I jolted. I don't know why, or how it would have helped, but my body burst with energy and fear and I was no longer in control. They expected it, though, and gripped me tight and my slight build was nothing to them.

"Clenching up is nice. Real nice. KEEP READING." Cray snarled, clearly first in line for me. My pants vanished, and someone's foot pressed against the back of my neck as something wet dripped down my anus.

He was spitting on me.

"KEEP READING, SON!" he called, voraciously gripping my hips. I felt him enter, and it hurt like nothing I'd ever known. He snarled, and I'm not sure what noises I made, but he was all the more encouraged by them.

"I can't see the book!" I pleaded, muffled and gasping for air as the leafy pages crinkled under my blood and tears.

"YOU KNOW THE NEXT LINE." he shouted, finding his cruel rhythm.

"Do onto others as you would have them do onto you!" I wept.

XIII

Albert Sergent

I don't think I've ever been this tired before. I can barely keep my eyes open. Gotta think of something else. I loved my brother, Sean, and moments like these I wish he were here. I once closed a car door on my hand and I cried. I must have been, what, six maybe? And he opened the door, pulled me out, and looked after me. He was always looking out for me.

I could really use that right now, but I guess it all works out. When he needed me most, I wasn't there either. Neither of our faults, I guess it's just how it works.

Sean had about two years and several inches on me. I was always scraping knees and picking up bugs where he was much more comely and presentable. He also had the eyes that looked like the sky before a storm in summer. Girls went crazy for him, and by the time he was fifteen he had neighborhood fame. Eighteen-year-old girls, blonde or brunette or whatever, would come in small groups knocking on the door to see if he could come out. They loved him. He made them laugh and my brother had this amazing ability not only to listen, but to make you feel as though you ought to be listened too. Sean was good like that. Good listener. Good confidant.

Well, one day when some of these girls were combing the streets for him, they found him. We lived in a poorer part of town, and they found him in a favorite hideaway in an abandoned apartment building. It was the kind of place that was decorated with beer bottles, condoms, and discarded clothes. It was where people did things they'd rather not speak of or take home the smell of.

And there Sean was, kissing another boy. I forget what happened to the other kid for the life of me. Can't even conjure up his name. Started with a 'B' I think but hell, I can't be sure. Anyway, they found him and got to making fun of him and mocking him and this other boy ran away sobbing and Sean stood his ground, saying that he simply 'liked' this other boy and kissed him. The girls, as playground legend had it, asked if he enjoyed it. He responded in the affirmative.

Many mothers called our house to make sure we knew of the offense. It was like they were calling us to tell us that someone had died. A few offered their sympathies and I even remember there being a cake baked for us by someone. Kids didn't knock on our door anymore, though. Horrible things were said about us and what happened within the walls of our house. I beat up my fair share of taunting boys because of it. Despite being small and young, I was good in a tussle. Still am.

My father was somewhat removed from the whole thing. I could tell he wanted to say something because he had the look of someone who was about to tell you to check your fly, but decided not to. Mom was different. She was very proactive and we went to help groups and Sean spent some time in state funded rehab clinics to cure him of the gay. He got in trouble at one of them, and was sent home. No one told me what happened, despite my constant top-of-my-lungs demands to know.

All of us stopped talking. "It's alright if you're a homosexual." I told him, not because I believed it, but because I just wanted him to feel better. Truth is I was angry at him. Furious even. He had done this to the family. But as angry with him as I was, I would never show it. The less and less my parents spoke to him, the more compelled I was to. I started sleeping on his floor, and we'd stay up late gazing at the glow-in-the-dark stars stuck to his ceiling while talking about the nature of mankind.

This is where my greatest education took place. I argued, as young as I was, that a place without religion would be a safer place for him to move to. His response was that secular government was capable of just as much hatred, and he taught me about Hitler and Stalin and Saddam as illustrations supporting this. I told him that even though he liked boys, maybe if he didn't act on it everyone would leave him alone. He told me that it was now permanent record, and besides, how is a man judged? By his desires or by his actions?

Then came my final question.

"What's it like... being a homosexual?" I was so uncomfortable asking, but I had to. Finding boys attractive was so alien to me, especially when girls were so pretty.

"I think it has a lot to do with God, and Adam. God made Adam in his own image, and so Adam is what God looks like. I... I love the male body, I like boys, so I guess I love God's image. Women do too, so I've got half the planet backing me on this one."

That last bit was an example of his classic humor.

"Why would God hate you for loving his body?"

"I'm certain, *certain* that God doesn't hate me. Most people seem to, though. Maybe it's because they are expected to hate me. Maybe they hate what I do. I don't know, but if God hated me I'd be able to tell."

And that's how it went. We moved a lot, and Mom and Dad worked in random jobs that made them sore at the end of the day. We never ate together at the dinner table either. We'd all just hit the kitchen at random times and nibble. The last place we moved to was here, Washington DC, and I was becoming a young man at that time.

I was about sixteen when it happened. Some cop spread the word about Sean and several kids welcomed me to the neighborhood by strapping me down onto a workbench and extinguishing matches between my toes. They stuck me with needles and stuffed things in my mouth like their socks and a condom one of them had found. They said all I had to do was cry up to God, not just for mercy or deliverance, but to strike my brother down. Not even when they took a pair of bolt cutters to my fingers did I do any such thing.

They were afraid that I'd die if I took anymore, so they let me go. I gimped home, my bloody lump of a hand wrapped in my shirt. Sean was the first to see me when I came through the door, and in his eyes at first glance he blamed himself. He rushed to me, frantic and helpless. Bleeding and having endured horror it was ironic that it was I who comforted *him*. I hushed him, told him it was okay, and that I was so glad that he was my brother and no one else. And I meant it. I still do.

But my mother screamed at him. "This is your fault, you sick twisted pervert of a child! I am disgusted that you came from my body!" I can still hear her screeching it, the festering cooze that she was may she burn.

I went to the hospital, and they kept me overnight. My mother wouldn't let Sean come and see me. At home he killed himself, and he did a good job of it. He had crammed half a jar of peanut butter down his throat before my father caught him. The paramedics only got creamy goodness when they tried to unblock his airway, and we held no service for him. There is no tombstone, no body, and I was never told what was done with the ashes.

Sometimes I don't feel that the world, after that particular day, is real. I took to cutting myself soon after it happened, just so I could feel something. I wanted to see the agony of Sean missing from my life. I wanted to see that damage on my surface heal, hoping that maybe deeper injury would heal the same way.

Such peculiar behavior brought me some attention, and when questioned by Civil Seraphim I registered as an atheist. After all, no god would ever let that happen to Sean. No god worthy of my worship anyhow. I joked with the Civs, told them I was glad that I still had my middle finger so that God could sit on it and spin until he squealed like two pigs on honeymoon.

Maybe there's some coffee around here to wake me up, but I'm too tired to look. This kitchen is pretty complicated looking. Type A family lives here.

Anyhow.

I have the background of a criminal, a monstrous story that makes swell news, and the face of an enemy, apparently. When Mueller died, a man I'd never met, it was surreal yet totally acceptable that I was to be blamed for his death. They must keep a database of misfits like me to resort to whenever they need a quick fix.

But when they came for me at my home, they probably weren't expecting the fight they got. My favorite was the bomb filled with rusty nails at knee level on the stairs. Up they came, in full battle gear swinging their assault rifles, stomping away and KA-BAM! After a few seconds of silence they started screaming and crying. I panicked them. See, that's what happens when you're at the top of the sociological food chain. You get cocky with us proles.

I ran from place to place, and to be honest Civil Seraphim's shock troops are none too shocking. I think they've gotten a bit lazy, polishing their Halloween costumes instead of training. I think they wanted a manhunt on their hands. Think about it. I run, cause some destruction, create a compelling story, and finally I get caught by "The Lone Archon" and his three stooges. My menace is neutralized, the public once again saved by The United States of Christendom.

All because some guy had the good sense to put a gun to his head and end it. Or so I heard in The Post. A lot of people keep saying that he was shot. Who knows? Personally, I think it was suicide simply because if you are going to assassinate someone, Mueller was a piss poor target to pick from what I've read about him.

Over the years I've educated myself in all things possible, and I learned something about revolution. I learned that the humanitarian... the flighty bastard with the beret and poetry book who swears allegiance to the underground is the first one to die. He buys it fast because, aside from being an idiot, he's missing the point behind conflict. To win a conflict, you must do what your enemy can't or *won't*. In short, you have to be more psychotic than the current psycho in power. No idealists, no Les Mis-whatever, no banging on the drums. You have to fight fire with more fire. But that leaves nothing but ashes. Thankfully, that's where the good people come in. They have the patience to sift through the ashes and get to work. Me, I couldn't build anything. No woman ever loved me and I was humane enough to never have children.

And so here I am, sitting in a stranger's kitchen. This town home is seasonal and I used to crash here for the summer. I was never greedy or messy, and they had never caught on that their space had been borrowed. Thankfully they have good cigars and given the circumstances I've finally helped myself to one. Eight boxes of cigars in a humidor but not so much as a first aid kit. Would you believe that? I've patched myself up as best I could though. The knick on my shoulder doesn't concern me so much so long as it doesn't get infected. My thigh, however, is starting to worry me. I keep compressing it and it just won't quit bleeding. Half the floor is covered with bloody paper towels and I'm almost out of clean bathroom towels. And the kitchen tile being white makes for a gruesome scene. I think one of those bastards shot me with a .357.

Man, am I tired.

Lysander seemed like a decent fellow, from the few sermons of his I peeked in on, and I hate to think that I led him to a poor fate. I told him I had killed Mueller, because anyone thinking or even breathing otherwise would find themselves in trouble. I hope he's okay.

Not Mueller, Lysander I mean. I liked him. Good people. Did you know that out of all bi-gender species, only humans and a closely related variant of ape persecute the homosexual? What does that tell you, eh? Anyway a biblical fundamentalist puts that in their pipe; they're still puffing some bitter tobacco.

Alright, enough. I'm just beat, dog tired. Think I'm going to rest while I can. I'm just so damned dead tired.

XIV

Thomas Hung

I had never been on a boat for so long before. There was no power, no radio, and I had even dunked my phone overboard into the river. After three days of listening to the water lapping while being rocked gently to sleep, I had made up my mind to spend the rest of my life on a boat.

Too bad I had no idea how to drive one. Don't get a romantic notion of me standing proud, leaning out over the stern on the high seas. I had spent the past three days hiding on one of Anne's family boats docked off of the Occoquan River just southwest of DC. I didn't have the keys for the thing, and it was one of the smaller yachts my future in-laws owned. Still, at 43 feet it was comfortable and the bed was surprisingly snug.

I didn't even mind the lack of power, warm food, or a working toilet. The chemical toilet suited me fine, and I simply rinsed it out every night in the river's water.

After the shock of what Robert had done had eased, I gradually began to panic. They would come for me. I was at Mueller's side for God's sakes, so it was clear that even if they believed I hadn't written the article they'd assume I had been involved. My future was very, very dim.

So I figured a docked boat belonging to Anne's family estate would be the safest place until I could figure things out. After a frantic grocery run, I took the city bus here, broke the lock on the yacht's door, and made myself at home with the curtains drawn.

The town of Occoquan is small and casual, like a tiny pocket of Americana cloistered by the river from an ocean of suburbia, so not only was my refuge out of the way, but it was charming. By the second day my panic had subsided. Maybe it was the birds overhead or the waves slapping against the hull, but I found myself thinking more and more about my life in general. How long had it been since I'd had a vacation? When was the last time my phone wasn't in my pocket? Had I ever spent an entire day not speaking before?

It was heaven! But I knew it couldn't last. Tomorrow I would have to go out and buy more food, and I had a limited amount of cash on me, so this wouldn't last forever. My bread was gone as were all the canned goods, and I was down to my last jug of water. It turns out I am awful at rationing. I suspect I'm a nervous eater. Someone would eventually come looking, perhaps even Anne or her parents, and the jig would be up. I was delaying the inevitable, and when they found me I had no idea what I was going to say.

On the third night I decided to dip into the three bottles of South African Paarl wine. There was something morose about being drunk, alone, and desperate and that seemed like exactly the place I wanted to be.

Halfway through the second bottle of wine, the door on the yacht opened. In ducked Anne's father, casually dressed in a sport coat and white button-up, beard trimmed perfectly as usual, with a twinkle in his eye. He saw me instantly, nodded knowingly, and sat in the cushion across from me at the small dining table.

"Hello, Thomas. You don't look too good."

I was drunk enough to where every gesture I made was tenfold. I flopped my hands in the air in mock despair.

"Ya GOT me." I confessed.

"Anne has been worried sick about you."

"Anne hash been worried sick about anythin and everthin."

"Why don't you love my daughter, Thomas?"

The question threw me for a loop. I was stunned at the candor of it, and the man asked it as though I had done him wrong.

"What do you mean?" I asked, swiftly sobering up from the hurt in his voice.

"She is the kindest, most tender woman on this planet yet you do not love her. It doesn't make sense to me. There are so many other men that would treat her better, but she loves you and I just don't know why."

"Anne... Anne is..." my train of thought wasn't boarding at the station. Wait, Anne actually loved me?

"Anne is too good for you, much like how my wife is too good for me. But we can't understand why women love us. I do not understand why Anne loves you. She hasn't eaten, her eyes are sunken, and she is doing everything in her power to find you."

Finally finding my words, I croaked out a minimal 'sorry' like a pathetic kid caught cheating at a board game.

"Honestly, I was hoping you wouldn't be here. I was hoping I couldn't find you, and then she could have her heart broken, rebuild, and move on to a man who would love her in return. I don't want to see her taken advantage of, and I don't want to see my grandchildren grow up in a home without love."

The table wasn't big enough for me to crawl under and hide.

"But here you are. Hiding on our boat, drinking our wine, and smelling exactly like a three-day-old uninvited guest would."

He stared at me for a long time. Knowing that this was the end, and there were most likely police on the dock waiting for me, I went back to the wine. "Well, when I get locked up forever I'll be sure to not accept her visits or write her." I simply did not care for pretense anymore.

"I don't care if you had anything to do with The Post scandal. I know you are no assassin, and to that end I've brought this…" He produced from his pocket an envelope and with a swift gesture it glided across the table to my hand. "It is your alibi and statement. It details how you and Robert Koss argued in his office and how he threatened you regarding your writing the story on Mueller's death. You were afraid, fled to this boat, and left a message for me to contact the authorities. A message, I might add, that I accidentally overlooked until after this conversation is over. I'll look like a fool, you'll look like a coward, but in the end you'll be fine and Anne won't have to pine for you from afar."

I'm pretty sure I blinked at this point in time.

"Well?" he asked, eyebrow playfully cocked. "Will you take the out I offer?"

My fingers fumbled with the envelope, opening it up and spreading it flat onto the table. Craning my head down to read it, Anne's Father suddenly became a whole new man to me. He had thought of everything, and every question I would be asked. Each detail for me to memorize was in bullet point form. The man was a far more artful liar than even me.

"Yeah. Yeah… I'll take it."

"There are conditions." His voice had found new volume and resolve. "You now will be respectful and kind to my daughter. You will treat her *right*. No more yo-yoing her around and no more being aloof."

I nodded like a chastised child.

"Additionally, you will run errands for me without question. They will be small, but vital and you will never speak of them to anyone or ask me about them afterward, is that understood?"

"You have a side business going on-"

"You don't get to ask questions, Thomas. You will memorize that envelope, dunk it in the chemical toilet afterward, and then turn yourself in at this address at this time to a man named Gabriel Wall." A small piece of paper came from his jacket in much the same manner as the envelope. This time I was sober enough to see the handle of a pistol under there as well. "He is the head of the investigation into Mueller's death and high up in Civil Seraphim. If you turn yourself in to anyone else, *that's* on you."

Sliding sideways from the table, he stood above me taller than ever. "Tomorrow will be very different for you. And the day after that. I expect you to keep your end of the bargain. Most important is that you treat Anne right. I don't know if you're even capable of love, but you will be the best man for Anne this Earth has. Got it?"

I nodded rapidly.

"Sober up, son. Clean up my boat, and do what you need to." He gave a second knowing nod, but this time without the twinkling eyes. As he ducked to leave I think the wine found its grip again.

"*My* boat…"

He paused, hand on the doorway. "What?"

"It's my boat now. I want this boat."

"Seriously?"

"Yes."

"Do you even know anything about boats?"

"Not a thing."

"They are a huge responsibility."

"I had a turtle as a kid."

He remained silently stupefied.

"I want this boat. I'm going to live on this boat." I pressed. The man's shoulders slumped. If I was to be a son-in-law I figured I'd start acting like one.

"Fine." He exhaled and left.

XV

Lysander Nikodemus

I bled considerably. I didn't know who to speak to about my bloody briefs or jumpsuit, but I quickly deduced it wiser to say nothing and hope for the best. Despite the toilet paper being thin enough to read through, I managed to stop my bleeding by wadding it up and packing my underwear with it.

Lurching crookedly, I shuffled my way in line to get breakfast. As it was flopped on my tray that familiar tree-trunk of an arm flopped over my shoulders. I winced at the extra weight, my visible pain eliciting sympathy from Cray.

He patted my chest with an insincere hand. "You fine, son. You fine. You my son now, *our* son. You fine. Nobody gonna hurt you. Holy Roller." He flashed his smile, and hovered near me as escort to his table. I was quickly wedged between him and the notched man, and as soon as my tray settled on the concrete table surface he helped himself.

With my meager feast picked clean, I stared intently at the center of the table in an effort to turn invisible while the men rowdily joked and jostled about as they ate. As they became more animated, they spoke more in tongue than English, almost strictly resorting to euphemisms and obscure prison nomenclature. A knowing glance would be shot to me on occasion, followed by a round of school yard snickers.

Cray was clearly proud to show off his new toy, and his energetic body was constantly in my space, jarring me out of my peaceful trance of oblivion.

Surrounded by him and his goons, they guided me into the commons area after breakfast like I was a reluctant political official being marched to the press to confess by his security detail.

As the morning lurched on, I observed Cray and his social doings. Most feared him, and the other gangs either avoided him or gave him slow nods from their corners of the world. On the surface it would seem like a casual gathering of thugs passing the time with cards, grunts, gestures, and guffaws. Underneath there was a constant and self-aware power play, and even though the gambling chips were no greater than cigarettes, orange juice, and simple gestures of respect, the stakes were their lives.

A cheap clock, protected by a tiny bent wire cage, hung on the wall and it slowly ticked away the minutes of the longest morning of my life. I know, as a man saved by Christ's blood, I should be thankful for every minute, but that morning I pondered my suicide. I knew that it would be like this for every day that Cray wished it, and I would be endlessly raped into a withered shell of my previous self if he was given to his devices. I belonged to someone now, and they derived new pleasure in my possession.

Would my days be spent like this, sitting still as an awkward and limping trophy, wondering how I was going to ask permission to use the bathroom? The thought of a bowel movement filled me with anxiety.

It was Cray's second chess game of the day, and he played against a silent member of the Cult of Mary. While having no overt evidence, the fact that a crowd gathered led me to suspect that there was something substantial

awaiting the victor, or perhaps worse something
substantial awaiting the loser.

The game paused. Glances between the small crowd
of spectators were knowingly exchanged, and slowly the
men wandered off into their affiliated territories. Within
seconds, the gathering had evaporated. A moment later I
saw why.

The outer security door 'thunked' internally as it
unlocked, and in came two guards with clubs on their
belts. They spread out, and an older man with the air of
authority came in.

"Nikodemus! Nikodemus! Lysander Nikodemus
come forward."

I made to stand, but Cray's hand rested on my knee
under the table. I swallowed hard, and weighed my
options facing me. Should I defy Cray, and suffer the
consequence, or was this my chance to advocate and
possibly evade further abuse?

As I pondered, a fourth person entered behind the
floor manager and brushed him aside. Gabriel Wall, with
three suited Civil Seraphim behind him as his personal
guard, spotted me instantly. With a stern gesture he
pointed at me using his entire hand, all fingers extended
and together like his entire arm under his elbow had been
forged into a blade.

"You." he commanded. "Come with me."

Cray's hand slipped off my knee, and I stood with
the help of the sturdy game table. Having sat for so long,
my muscles had seized up from my clenching and I
lurched from my seat. I didn't look about, but I was
certain that all eyes were on me.

I took several agonizing steps toward Wall, and
from the disgusted fury on his face, it was easy to see he

perceived what my previous evening had been comprised of.

His pointed hand changed targets. "Him." He pointed at Cray. "I want him. He have friends?"

No one spoke. Wall glanced over his shoulder to his three men, and they leapt to life. Cray flashed his welcoming grin, elbow casually propped against his game table "We just playing chess, man. Is all good."

The three men in suits surrounded him, and I hadn't noticed it before but they all had brass knuckles on. Without a word, they beat him. It wasn't an angry beating, or even an enthusiastic one, but a brutal one. The first strike broke Cray's nose, knocking him off balance. The second and third both landed on the side and the top of his head as he was trying to crawl under the table. They lunged for him; a flurry of white-cuffed hands groped for his legs and pulled him back into the open.

Each other prisoner now pressed themselves against the walls and into the corners of the room, very much wishing to become invisible as I had desired earlier.

Wet thump after thump landed directly on Cray's face and head, rocking his skull about loosely on his shoulders. The sound of his cheek bones cracking and sinuses collapsing shivered my spine. Like travelling workmen, they pounded at him like a circus tent stake. Eventually out of breath, the three men slowed, stopped, stood, pulled out wipes for just such occasions and cleaned themselves off. One even straightened another's tie.

Cray splayed on his back, feet elegantly together yet arms skewed awkwardly like an improper crucifix, a bloody bubble rising and falling with his labored breath.

Wall turned his ire back to the floor manager. "You will transfer Nikodemus to where I told you."

"Of course, sir. But it was Mr. Howell that transferred him into the violent population in the first place."

"Will Mr. Howell come down here and visit you personally when something isn't as he likes it?" Wall's voice was barely above a whisper now, but its growl echoed.

The manager didn't dare respond.

"Get Nikodemus to the infirmary." Wall barked. "I want all of his paperwork through my office. Always."

The two guards swooped in on me, each careful to avoid eye contact with Wall's men or the bloody mess on the floor, and with their arms hovering behind me, they ushered me out.

XVI

Faith Wall

So, if God has made man in the image of himself, then what does it mean if I can't stand men? Does that mean I can't stand God? Most people need a slap in the face, so would I be slapping God? Ugh.

Our after school pledge states to 'hold the bible in our hearts to keep from sinning against God' so does that mean I am sinning against God when I'm angry with boys or men? God is a 'he' after all. It's like I'm boxed in! I can't express my anger toward anyone without coming off like I don't belong. It's like the bible was written just to make me feel bad. I'm a girl, and every single woman in the bible is a whore, a victim, or the bad guy.

Doubt me? Well, let's look!

Eve. Eve is an idiot. A talking snake gets her to convince Adam to eat a bad apple. God shows up demanding answers, Adam immediately points at Eve, and that's that. I don't buy that for a second. My mother would in *no way* take an apple from a talking snake. She'd be all like 'why can't you give the apple to Adam yourself?' and 'thank you, but I don't take gifts from strangers, even friendly snakes.' Most likely Adam saw the apple, wanted it badly, and tried to get Eve to polish it for him and validate his hunger. We know how boys love apples.

How about Mary? No, not mother Mary or Mary Magdalene (she was possessed by demons, and needed a man to fix her) but whore Mary. Of Bethany. She gets by any way she can and let's be honest: no little girl says 'I want to be a whore when I grow up!' Seriously. Why are we blaming the victim? Men made sure that being a whore was her best option, and then when they are done with her or when their neglected wives get angry enough it's stoning time. They just want to sweep away the trash. Thank goodness Mary had a man, a *son* of God, to save her.

Mother Mary, then. She's a virgin and she gets pregnant. Did she ask God to make her pregnant? Did God have consent? Was there dinner and a movie first? Was God in the form of a bull or a swan like other rapist gods, or did he just make her sleep? Maybe slip something in her drink like Darius Thaxton tries to do at parties?

Women are in The Bible to make men cut their hair, lose their power, and tempt them. They're treated as rewards or taken as punishments. We get turned to salt for looking back to pity those that were shamed, and we are valued only for our ability to make children. If we don't have that, then making babies is outsourced to other women living in the house. And guess who still has to clean the house?

So why, with all of this, do I even believe and listen to a book and a religion and a dogma that has nothing but contempt for me, and all my lady parts? And I'm not even special enough for my god to rape me like Mother Mary.

But here's the thing, I know God exists. I know it. I felt it as a little girl. I feel it when I watch my mother in the kitchen and I feel it when I spy on my father as he sits at the kitchen table when he gets home at three in the morning. I feel God in the color purple and in small acorns and I smell God in a freshly cut lawn. God is in old people's knuckles and in the songs of birds and in the air just before a thunderstorm. I see God in all kinds of paintings and artworks on walls and from books in the library. It's usually the nature paintings, not the *actual* paintings of God.

I saw God in a stray cat once. It had no tail and I think it had mange, but God was in those eyes. God looked at me for a moment then scampered off under a car. It's how my relationship with God tends to go, I think.

Know what? I bet God didn't make 'man' in his image. I bet God made otters in his, or ITS, image. The day of the otter will rise and the King James Bible will be the first book in the Great Otter Doctrine. God seems better suited for a bristly-mustached little otter banging a clam on a rock than it does a man. Know why? Because when that little bit in me feels God it is the exact same feeling I get when I look at an otter: fuzzy, warm, comforting, and charming. *That* is God. Whiskery, adorable, and easily overlooked.

XVII

Rosa McPhearson

It was after lunch, and I noticed Howell's glance avoiding mine throughout the late morning. Something was off, and I couldn't get his questions about Finny out of my head.

I had to see my boy. I'm sure you've been there before. Every parent has.

I called his school. Just to make sure Finny was doing okay. He was in class taking a quiz, and all seemed fine according to the chipper lady on the phone. Despite that, I needed to actually *see* him. During the Monsignor's Archon meeting to discuss Sergent, I drove to the school. My heels clomped through the hall loudly, reminding me of how awkward I felt in the boys' school.

A chubby administrative assistant walked me to his classroom door and I peered in. His little head was bent down; hand furiously writing away as he solved equation after equation. Other children huffed and rolled their eyes and whimpered to themselves in self-pity. One was even visibly praying.

"He's doing just fine. Finney's grades are fantastic, as well as his conduct. He's a model student and well mannered! He always says please and thank you!" the chubby lady said. We shared a smile, she sharing my pride. "And you'll be pleased to know that his appointment this morning went fantastic with the nurse."

Appointment? Nurse? I figured it to be school

inoculations. But usually they send a form home…

"Most children scream and scream and scream when they get their blood taken, but not Finny." she continued.

"Blood taken? Why did he need to have his blood taken?"

"For the doctor. We faxed the records early this morning. Did your husband ask for it, do you think?"

I was utterly confused. "What was the doctor's name?" I asked, mounting horror building in my voice, though not sure why. My brain hadn't caught up with my instinct yet.

"You know, I can't remember. Susan sent the fax off herself, so we should go ask her." I don't remember walking back to the office. I know I made conversation on the way, but I can't recall what about. I shook someone's hand eventually, and heard the name of the Monsignor's doctor spoken.

I don't know how I might have appeared after hearing his name, but I suspect I was like a forgotten pot boiling pasta on the stove. My lid was rattling and I might have been frothing. I had met my final breaking point. This was the final transgression. I had been violated endlessly and shamelessly and now he was going to violate my son with blood being taken by a doctor he owns?

No.

"I'm going to go ahead and take him home, now." I said as calmly as possible, my hands together to keep from trembling with rage. "I'd like him dismissed from class and released to me, please."

I think I thanked them. I'm not sure. Finny soon arrived, his backpack nearly as large as his body, and he beamed at me when our eyes met in the office. Even in public, and even as he grew close to the age where it was unmanly for a boy to adore his mother, he still gave me the most genuine and deep hugs every time.

Walking to the car, my vision darted all over in heightened awareness around the lot. Every slamming car door in the distance was suddenly a threat and my boy was too excited to be out of school early to be vigilant. I was like a mother and her cub in a forest full of hunters.

"Where are we going?" Finny chirped as he climbed into the back seat.

"Today, I thought, should be a special day since your friend Allen has school off. All county schools do. So maybe you'd like to go visit him for a bit?"

"Really!?"

"Really."

At the first stop light, I desperately dialed Allen's mother, Darlene. She had always been a charming and friendly woman who curses just enough for you to trust her without her coming off as vulgar.

She picked up, thank God. "Heya! How are things?" I did my best not to sound strained.

"What's the matter, Rosa?" Darlene could somehow tell instantly. "You alright?"

"Yeah, um, listen. I was hoping Finny and Allen could spend some time together this afternoon. Would that be alright?"

"Honey, anything you need. Need him to spend the night?"

I tilted the mirror so that Finny wouldn't see my eyes welling up with tears. I began breathing deeper, trying to hold in the squeaking sob that was building in me.

"Sweetie, anything you need. You bring Finny on over here, I've got an extra toothbrush and I'll take them to the movies. It will be a sleepover and I'll take the boys for a movie and pizza. You don't need to worry about a thing. What about Finny's brother?"

Gathering myself enough to sound normal, I finally responded. "He'll be fine. He's fine. I was just hoping Finny could spend some time with you and Allen if that's alright."

"Of course. Just come on over."

Darlene couldn't have been more accommodating. As soon as we arrived Finny shot upstairs to Allen's room and Darlene had a warm cup of tea waiting for me. She didn't ask questions, but having been through a rough patch with her husband she was sensitive not to dive too deeply into my apparent misery.

We sipped tea, talked about the boys, and each time Darlene gave me a knowing stare, I kept my eyes down. "Thanks. Don't worry about having him call me to say goodnight. I want the boys to have fun."

Darlene nodded, accepting my pathetic reasoning not to be disturbed.

"Just..." I hesitated. "Just don't tell anyone he's here until tomorrow, if you could? It's complicated."

Without hesitation, Darlene nodded in acceptance.

I struggled to give her a grateful smile without crying, stood to leave, and hugged her tighter than I expected. Darlene and I had always been friendly, but for the first time I realized how kind she was, and she was there for me.

"I'll let them know you're leaving."

"No..." I interrupted. I knew that if I saw Finny I would burst into tears. I couldn't break down. I had to be leaving before rush hour traffic kicked in. After all, I had a man to murder before dinner.

I had kept Finny from the Monsignor for fear that he would recognize him as his own son. That's why there are no pictures on my desk, or in my purse. That's why we stopped coming to the Christmas and Easter parties years ago.

Up to this point, I had been in denial. I had just hoped that somehow, magically, Finny would live a full life without anyone becoming the wiser. I'd needed it to stay my personal, dark family secret. If, in my autumn years, it came out to Teddy he would forgive me because after all we had such a beautiful son.

I had no doubt in my mind that the Monsignor would make Finny vanish; no Monsignor of such a high station could violate his Catholic oath of celibacy in such a manner as to have a child with a married woman. It would be the end of his career, and the Catholic Church itself would make an example of him for every other Catholic bishop in public official to see.

Finny was in mortal danger by the director of Civil Seraphim. I've worked there long enough to know what paperwork gets lost and why.

Could I talk to the Monsignor? Call him 'Michael' and tell him how wonderful Finny is? Could I convince him that someone special came from something disgusting, and half of the blood in my boy's veins was his own? Maybe the Monsignor would come out to the public, admit fault, and while I would be hounded into oblivion like a whore of Babylon, Finny would live. What man could make his own son vanish?

I had no one to go to, no means of defense, and I was certain there was no one to help me. I drove in circles, around and around until the afternoon was half spent. In my mind the Monsignor's face was vivid, in the throes of his savage passion as he stood over me, hand around my throat while the other one gripped and twisted my nipple until it bled. I had to incorporate chokers and high collars into my wardrobe because of that man. I had to use tear-resistant mascara because of that man. I had to hide my nipples and shoo away my husband from my breasts because of that man.

Something built up inside me, something that had been begging to come out for ages. I stopped by a grocery store and looked at all the knives with a furious rage and evil joy. I found one, suitable for carving off the Monsignor's face. It was serrated and thick at the bottom, surely not to break during repeated stabbing. It had a flower on the handle, sure to match with an apron for any Susie Homemaker to wield in the kitchen.

When I finally returned to the office, I was walking taller than I think I ever have, but I still slipped in without much notice. The Monsignor's door was slightly ajar, a clear indication that he was in. He kept it closed and locked otherwise.

Creeping to my desk, I set my purse down slowly and pulled the knife out. I then stood perfectly still, listening intently. Hearing nothing, I figured him to be reading. Trying to conceal the blade under some papers I was carrying, I walked full-bore into the room. The only way to get close to him was for him to peer over my shoulder at something in my hands. He likes that. He likes to smell me that way.

"Sorry I'm late, I just-" When I entered I saw that his chair was vacant. I stopped dead in my tracks, and spun about to see Gabriel leaning against the bookcase behind me, hands folded in front of him with his head bowed. I couldn't read his face but it was particularly cold, those metal eyes of his distant.

"Stabbing between the second and third rib is the best way for a silent kill. It gives them no chance to scream. If you give it a twist and retract, you take apart the lung and they drown in blood." he said matter-of-factly while nodding to my knife. The papers must have slipped from my fingers when I saw Gabe.

A long silence passed.

"Drop it." he commanded. I pointed the blade at his chest and backed away.

"He's going to take my son!" I screamed, my own voice ringing my ears. Gabriel didn't flinch. "That *thing* is going to hurt Finny! You'll take me away, but he can't hurt Finny!"

"If word gets out that he isn't celibate, his career is over and the entire Seraphim will be distrusted as a source of scandal. Vigilance is our reputation." He looked away from me to the window. "I'm not sure what will happen to your boy. I haven't been told yet."

It was too much. Too much. I wanted the horror to make me faint, to drop me into an empty place of forgetting so that when I awoke the terror will be over and only sorrow would remain.

"Don't let him kill Finny!" I pleaded, my words warped with an erupting sob. I dropped the knife without thinking, ran forward, gripped Gabe by the collar, and shoved him. He made no contest against me, letting me thrash him about. "He's a good boy! He's kind, and loving and full of Godliness and this filthy world needs him!" I yanked Gabe down to my height and got right into his face. I was barely able to see him through my blurring tears, but I could make out those eyes, bright and burning through to me. "At the Christmas party after he was first born you saw him. Remember? He was in my arms and you saw him! You will not let this happen!"

"Mrs. McPhearson, whether he lives or dies is not up to me. If he is to die, then whoever does it... will just do it. There's nothing anyone can do about it."

I fell to my knees, hands pulling my hair, crying uncontrollably, praying to God to spare my child. My youngest boy. Gentle Finny.

Gabriel let me do so. He gave me, I think, about fifteen minutes or so. I can't really be sure. He just stood there, thinking, until my crying eased a bit.

"It's time to go. We have a drive ahead of us." he said.

Swinging the office door wide, he stepped out; his open palm gesturing me forward like a butler. His three underlings had found their way into the office lobby and had spread out, leaning against the wall or slouching in furniture. They collectively devoured me with their eyes.

One gripped my elbow.

"We're taking the private elevator to avoid a scene. No scenes, missy." one of them said to me. The descent into the echoing concrete garage was timeless, and I was a passenger in my own body. The three men enveloped me, one in front, one to my side, and one behind. I could feel Gabriel far behind me. I wished he were closer.

They walked me to two black sedans. The one grasping my elbow looked to Gabriel.

"She's with me, in the back seat." he said.

"No, she isn't." Gabriel replied flatly while pushing through the three men and opening the back door.

Nobody moved.

"Rosa, please get in." Gabriel said, somewhat annoyed.

"I want to sit up front." I wasn't trying to be childishly difficult, but it was the only way I could think of to grab the steering wheel if I got the chance. I was already surrounded by men and powerless. I had to have *something*.

"Rosa..." He could barely keep his annoyance from betraying his calm demeanor. "Please get into the back seat of this car."

I did so. The door shut behind me, and the three men stood by themselves chatting tersely for a moment. With Gabriel unmoving, they eventually all piled into the other car.

I went to toy with the locks quietly, but found there were none. Not even a handle. In front of me was a polished Plexiglas barrier to keep me from climbing into the front seat.

The driver's side door opened and Gabriel slid in, shut his door, turned his key, and backed out of the spot.

"You met Finny at the Christmas party that one year. He was only a few months old." I said, reminding him. I had to place a picture of my boy in his mind.

He began driving but said nothing. Behind us, never more than a car's length away, were the Three Stooges.

I wondered where we were going. Were they going to drive me to a prison? A hospital of some kind? Home? Was I going to see the Monsignor in some private place so he could try and talk me into something? Was I to sign something? Would the Monsignor demand a confession, or simply want his way one last time before sending me off to the bottom of a river?

I hoped that if they killed me, they'd let Finny remain a secret. Perhaps my death was the only one warranted. Maybe down the road the Monsignor would open doors for him from afar? Maybe the Monsignor would discover his fatherly instinct?

I got tired of wondering. Wiping my eyes, I composed myself as best as I could in the reflection of the car window.

"What are you going to do to me?" I demanded with more force than I felt. "If you kill me, you don't have to kill Finny. No one would ever know."

Gabriel remained silent.

I decided to go fishing.

"How are you going to kill me?" I asked, trying to provoke him into assuring me that it wasn't the case. Maybe I could infer the real plans from his response.

He sighed.

"Howell didn't specify." he finally said. I started to tingle all over and my lungs couldn't expand enough. I saw him adjust his rearview mirror to get a clear look at me.

I cried.

"And what about my son!? Did Howell specify what was to be done with him!?" I screeched. "If you kill me, Finny can get away! No one else knows! I swear to God, no one else knows! Just kill me, I won't fight, but leave Finny alone!"

"I told you. I don't know what will happen with Finny. That's not up to me. That isn't me."

"So, you don't kill children?"

He had no response for that.

"Is that where you draw the line? Archons can take women, civilians, whomever, but not children? They can take peaceful priests and reverends but not children? Does the paperwork on killing kids run through someone else's office? How fortunate you are to be so far removed from that particular horror!"

"There's always someone more than willing to work their way up the ladder, even if it means killing you or a child. If I don't, someone worse will. With you I can at least make it painless and... respectful."

"Bullshit!"

"Someone else would do it. *They* would do it."

"They!?"

"They. Someone. There is always someone."

We were getting farther out of the city now, heading South on the interstate. I stared off into space, occasionally looking behind us to keep an eye on the car following: its driver and passengers stoic behind their sunglasses.

A while passed. A long while. I thought of my parents, the muddy river waters of my childhood home, and I wondered if God would let me see Finny again. I realized I hadn't thought much about my husband Teddy, or other son Martin, for that matter. I felt a flush of crushing guilt because I had worried so much about Finny. Was Finny my favorite? Would I be as upset about losing Martin as Finny? How would Teddy cope with it all? Would my body be missing? Would he wonder where I was? Would Martin grow up broken? And Finny, if he remains untouched by all this?

"Where's mommy?" he would ask.

The car finally came to a stop on a dirt road off of some larger dirt road in Stafford. Maybe this was the place for this kind of wet work.

Gabriel turned around in the driver's seat and looked at me hard, and without pity.

"This will not hurt." he said.

I pointed to the other car as it pulled out around us and parked facing ours. Daylight was dimming and the setting sun stabbed through the trees casting lines of gold onto the three men inside.

"Which of them will be asked to kill my son? Which of them will get your job for doing so?" I asked, my tears exhausted and my voice croaking.

Gabriel got out, walked to my door, opened it and took my elbow.

"Do everything I tell you to." he said sharply, lifting me up and walking me in between both cars facing each other. He looked about on the ground and stood me in a spot, pressing my arm downward as if to fix me there. Stepping back he drew a pistol. It wasn't his usual pistol. I can figure on why.

I looked him dead in the eye, and didn't allow a single sniffle. "It will never stop, you know. It won't ever stop. He'll get another secretary and do as he pleases and then you'll have to kill her too. Her children will also go missing. And will you just keep wiping your hands clean of it?"

"Kneel." he said softly.

"I'd rather stand." I tried to say, but my lips moved without sound.

He looked annoyed, and glanced to the men casually lounging in their car in front of us, arms dangling out of open windows, watching the show.

Gabriel put his right foot back, stepped forward with his left, and rested his pistol into both his hands. He looked at me hard, but dispassionately.

Was this how Gabriel Wall looked before he killed? Apparently it was.

XVIII

Gabriel Wall

Colt M1911A1 ten round magazine, one chambered. Eleven rounds, alternating hollow point and hardpoint. Must lean in to keep from jamming. Hands cool, not sweaty, heartrate smoothish.

Dammit, Rosa. You'd better duck.

First round, hollowpoint, through driver's side glass shattering visibility. Driver, Fendrick, most likely hit in throat.

Relocate. Two steps left.

Fire three rounds into front passenger. Aim low. He's ducking. First round shoulder, other two sternum.

Relocate. Five steps. Passenger side window.

Rosa screams. Ignore.

Two more rounds into passenger. Take his fight.

Relocate. Two steps back to rear seat window. Expect firearm drawn.

Firearm NOT drawn! Third crawling into floor space to save own hide! Abandoned allies! Didn't defend! He had a chance at me!

ANGRY.

Remaining rounds into third on car floor.

Weapon spent. Eject clip. Leave on ground. Do not care anymore.

Relocate. Around back of car. Driver's side door. New magazine.

Open door. Fendrick wounded directly in throat. Hands clasping it, blood pouring from mouth like he ate someone. Eyes begging for mercy.

Round chambered. Mercy given.

XIX

Rosa McPhearson

Everyone has seen the movies, and the television shows, where people shoot at each other. This was nothing like that. There was a lot more smoke than I expected, it was deafening, and everything happened so quickly. It wasn't a gunfight like on the police shows, it was an execution.

Gabriel slid his pistol back under his suit jacket, and walked to our car, popping the trunk. He began undressing.

All I managed to do was blink. Thinking back, I don't think I moved during the whole thing.

Tossing his suit jacket into the trunk, he pulled his shirt off, not even unbuttoning it. There were speckles of blood on the front and a splotch on his right collar. Soon he was in a sleeveless undershirt, unwrapping a freshly plastic-bound shirt and tie.

I finally found my wits, and looked back at the other car. It sat as black and as polished as a coffin, front window cracked, fragmenting the image of the men inside. The driver had his head slumped back, his throat open. Smoke drifted up from the whole scene like a campfire had water dumped on its ashes.

Gabriel must have seen me looking at him in horror.

"That one, the driver there, wanted your death to look like a sex crime. It was his excuse to rape you." he said, slightly out of breath as he fumbled with his cufflinks. His fingers trembled almost uncontrollably and he looked flustered. It was like his hands weren't his own.

Finally finding control over my body, and a euphoric sense of serenity, I walked over to him. Something in my body shifted, and a power surged through me. I remembered the polite yet distant Gabriel of my workplace, and helped him with his cuffs. Next his tie, and just like Teddy on a stressful morning he stood still, chin up, while I adjusted him.

"What happens now?" I asked.

He looked over at the car. "I'm not sure. This isn't how I wanted things to happen, but there it is." He fetched his suit jacket and closed his trunk. "We leave them. No point in hiding it. We'd lose too much time."

"What about Finny?" I asked, hope renewed.

He nodded understandingly, but instead of replying he pulled out a short, crescent-shaped knife from the other side of his jacket. Opening the driver's side door, he dug into the paneling around the steering column and tossed twisted slivers of plastic and faux leather into the grass. Finally, with a grunt and a jerk he lifted a small, unassuming black box from within the guts of the dashboard. Several wires hung out of it.

"This…" he said, putting the knife away. His hands were back under his control. "Was recording everything in the car and broadcasting it to the *other* car. I kept trying to drop you hints to relax, but I didn't want to push it too hard."

"Is there one in the other car?"

"Yes. I'm going to dig it out. These are used to track us as well."

"How long until they come looking for us?"

"Howell will give me my space to do his dirty laundry, so maybe a day. Or longer, since I'm the one who is usually sent out to check on these things. We're going to take these with us and dunk them into the Occoquan on our way back North."

I lit up. With a lurching hug I snatched at Gabriel. I must have ruffled his jacket and disheveled him because his returned embrace was so restrained.

"We're going to go get Finny!" I said, finding more tears. "Right?"

"We are going to meet up with them. I have a man that contacted Ted and explained everything. They should be ready to go soon. We just have to get you there. Getting there with you was my original intention, but Howell saddled me with these guys. Speaking of which, I still have to get the box out of their car."

It didn't take long. Then Gabe rolled the dead driver under the car to prevent the body from being seen from a distance.

I sat in the passenger seat of our car and waited. Silently he got in, shifted into gear, and we began the rumbly drive up the dirt road.

"We won't be travelling directly to your family." Gabriel added. "Two more people need to join you on your trip. We'll pick them up first."

"Where am I going?"

"Buenos Aries. It will be hard for anyone to follow you there, you know the land, and Argentina has withdrawn their ambassador from the US ever since the Mexican Police Action, so you should be secure."

"All four of us? My whole family will go?"

"Yes, together, by plane and by boat."

"What about you?" I asked, thinking about the orgy of evidence left at the other car, three dead men strewn about. Gabriel had no future here.

"What about me?" he replied.

"Where are *you* going?"

"Home."

XX

Faith Wall

So, Mom and I ate dinner together as usual. We chatted about how much trouble I had gotten into at school.

Apparently, Jesus has all his teeth and swims twice a day to maintain his washboard abs. I learned this because of the completely hilarious fuss my painting caused. The other kids were offended, stunned, and horrified and their parents called in demanding Ms. Clementine's head.

I was laughing the whole time, telling them to call Dad and yell at him for raising me so wrong. I *dared* them to. But they called Mom and Mom came and had a conference with the dean and Ms. Clementine.

That's when I got angry. It was clear that Dean Sanders didn't want trouble with Mom or Dad so he began by apologizing for the horrible lack of guidance that I had been given from Ms. Clementine! Apparently the assignment was poorly worded and unguided and the school was embarrassed and Dean Sanders swore up and down that he would never allow anything like this to happen again to me. TO ME!

I began yelling. I told Dean Sanders what I thought of him and his choice in ties, and then I railed him for blaming Ms. Clementine. I saw her in the corner seat, wide-eyed and listening to me rant about how she was not to blame and was the only tolerable person in their whole filthy back-stabbing school, and she just sat there trying to motion for me to calm down.

For me to calm down? Like a good, biblical woman should? Listen to the men, and not be taken seriously? To be blamed for other people's choices?

Eventually Mom held my hand, took it firmly, and said it was time to go. She also, God bless her, said she looked forward to working with Ms. Clementine in the future about my artwork assignments since Ms. Clementine is the reason why she, and Dad, were so pleased with the school overall.

Only my mother can calm me down. And apparently Dean Sanders. And Ms. Clementine even stopped crying for a bit. I think Mom saved her job.

We were handed my painting, and asked to take it home. I looked it over. Yep, Jesus was a fatty with wide-sagging man-boobs and tummy flab covering over his bathing-suit area. I gave him all his teeth though, but made them yellow from all the wine and fish he eats.

The best part is above Jesus in the clouds, encompassed with a holy nimbus, is a godly otter; tiny paws out and claws open, bestowing holy light down unto Golgotha. Praise be unto the whiskered one, He Who Is I Am, breaker of clamshells and sliding on His belly into warm summer waters.

I didn't even try to hide how proud I was of my painting as I held it up one last time for Dean Sanders to look at it. Here's hoping that image is burned into his mind while he sleeps and if it sneaks in just once during his prayers that means I won. I am in his mind, and he cannot unsee what I shoved in his face.

We ate dinner with the painting propped in the chair next to me.

"You know, you really are talented."

"I love drawing and painting." I said, low.

"It's okay to be proud." Mom said, her hand once again finding mine.

I felt ashamed suddenly. "Why do you guys put up with me? Well, you, at least. Why do you put up with me?"

"And not your father?"

"You're the one that always goes to do the meetings and teacher conferences and things like that. Dad is too busy, or can't be bothered to deal with me. Maybe I'm like a boy, trying to get into trouble to get his attention."

Mom listened thoughtfully, sipped her soup, and squeezed my hand before using it to take a drink of wine.

"I really don't think you're like a boy." she said with a smirk. "And besides, your father was delighted to hear that he would have a little girl. He was afraid that if he had a boy, the boy would be like him."

"Emotionally stunted?"

"Faith, that isn't nice."

"But it is fair. You guys have separate bedrooms. Do you honestly expect me to have any idea of what a marriage is when I get older... *this* being my example?" I regretted it the moment I said it.

Mom was clearly hurt. "Life does strange things to us sometimes, Faith. I didn't choose this for your father and me."

"Did he?"

"I'm not sure. He changed over time."

"I've seen your wedding pictures. I've seen all the pictures with you two together smiling when I was five or six."

"Those were much easier times."

"What happened, Mom?"

"Sweetie, just know your father loves you, and he isn't good at showing much of any emotions right now. But just know he loves you."

"Maybe I know it, Mom, but I don't feel it. I haven't felt it in a long time."

A door opened in the house. Mom instantly tensed up. "Hello?" she called. "Hello, is someone here? Gabe?"

She got up quickly, hand open toward me motioning for me to keep seated. Walking swiftly into the kitchen, she went out of my eyesight to check the back door.

I heard her gasp.

I was up instantly, running and frantic. Mom doesn't gasp.

Charging into the kitchen I saw Dad with another woman. She was worn out, her makeup a wreck. She was beautiful, though, and her beauty made her miserable state look twice as sad. Mom looked at her, then to Dad, then back at her. The puzzled look on Mom's face slowly faded.

"Is this it, Gabe? Is it us, now?"

Dad just nodded. Mom swallowed hard, stood tall, and looked to me.

"Go pack." she said. "We have about ten minutes."

"Someone is waiting in the car for us, too." Dad said, a hand at the strange woman's back as he pushed her forward a bit. "Rosa, this is my wife Kathy. And my daughter, Faith."

Rosa nodded. "Pleased to meet you." she said, with a startling sincerity. She looked like I did when Terrance Fishbourne broke up with me. He was such a jerk, but I cried anyway and then realized 'hey, he was a jerk!'

My brain finally began catching up. "Wait, pack?

Why? Where are we going?" I asked, a bit optimistic that I wouldn't have to go to school tomorrow.

"Away." Dad said. Mom took Rosa by the shoulder with both her hands.

"Who is in the car?"

"That's my boy, Finny. He's a bit younger than you. He's reading."

"Rosa, let's head upstairs. Maybe we can freshen up a bit and I bet we can find some clothes that fit you." Turning to me, and using a sterner voice, Mom spoke to me. "Faith, go pack."

Dad turned his back on us, opened the basement door, and creaked his way down the wooden stairs.

"Alright." I said, with no intention of doing a damned thing without getting answers first. "But I have to ask Dad something."

I bolted down the stairs before Mom could stop me. Even in these circumstances she worried about making a scene in front of a 'guest' and didn't yell after me. As I followed Dad, I heard the upstairs move and creak, meaning Mom had taken Rosa to her room.

"Dad?" I said, walking through the basement's boxes and dusty workout equipment. "Dad!"

The door to his private storage room was swung open, the metal lock dangling free. I never got to go in here.

Peeking in, I saw Dad reach up and switch on several lights.

"Yeah?" he said, sorting through some thick duffle bags on metal shelves.

"Dad, what is going on?"

"We're leaving the country. Mom, you, me, Rosa, and her family, too."

"But WHY!?"

He blinked at me. "Does it matter?" he finally said as he pulled a long rifle sheath from the wall. "Here." He said, pulling out a duffle bag. "This one is yours. Don't bring any clothes. Just go upstairs and pack a few personal things you can't live without."

It was heavy and dense, and a bit dusty. I dragged it out of the room into the clear of the basement floor and unzipped it. Socks, tooth paste, thin shirts, sneakers, and funny enough, a tin of drawing pencils and a pad of some really nice paper.

"I'll be right back." he said as strode over me, walking up the basement stairs with several bags over his shoulders. "Bring that to the kitchen table when you're ready. Be quick."

Dad packed me pencils? I peeked back into his storage room, finally getting a chance to be in his forbidden hideaway, and explored.

There was a padded stool, and also a long bench with two metal arms coming up from the center and some small tools on it. There were several lights on bendy arms overhead, so he must have tinkered here or something.

There were two pictures on the wall behind the bench. One was of Mom while she was sleeping. It didn't seem that long ago, since her hair in it is the same color as it is now. The other was a drawing of Dad's face I had done. I gave it to Dad for Christmas when I was eleven. I drew it from memory, without looking at him, just to test myself. The lines were childish, and he looked a bit cartoonish, but he still looked like he was giving his usual sad smile. It was as though he knew a truth that would depress you, but he'd rather keep it to himself and let you remain happy.

He always had that smile.

I walked out and picked up my duffle bag. I struggled with it up the stairs, and when I came to the kitchen I saw Dad sitting next to my flabby-Jesus painting, leaning forward looking at it.

I walked up next to him, and we examined it together.

"I got into trouble." I said.

"Good." he said.

"Do you like it?" I chanced.

"Faith, I *love* it. May I have it?"

"Sure."

"I'm going to bring it with us to keep it safe."

"Thanks."

Dad's attention suddenly turned toward me. "You will be safe, too." he said.

Rosa came downstairs looking like a new woman, with a suitcase in her arms filled with Mom's clothes. I grabbed several things vital to a teenage girl's life while Dad gathered the duffle bags and put them into the car. Mom put together road lunches as fast as possible. Dad also wrapped my painting with a thin blanket and cord. I felt like a third wheel.

We all piled into the car as if embarking on the tensest Sunday drive *ever*. I sat next to the boy, Finny, while Dad drove us to the docks at Occoquan River. Finny seemed like a nice boy, and he seemed to pretend that he didn't know what was going on, but I know a sharp kid when I see one. When she first entered the car, he lowered his Captain America comic book just enough to watch her like a hawk, more vigilant than the super hero holding the cross in one hand and the shield in the other.

A lot of rich folks have boats there, including a

friend of Dad's I hadn't heard of before named Thomas.

I had never met Thomas before, but I could tell he was nervous when we pulled up to the docks. Dad didn't even look at him, but introduced us while he was loading the boat with all of our stuff.

"You're going to another dock south of the inlet, and there you'll meet up with Ted and your other son. There's a bigger boat there, and you'll be fine." Dad said to Rosa and Finny with his usual sad smile.

Rosa nodded, her hand to her lips containing her overwhelming gratitude, and she hugged Dad. It was the kind of hug I didn't even see Mom give him anymore.

He hugged her back, but looked to Mom while doing so. After she finally freed Dad, Thomas helped Rosa and Finny onto the boat.

"How can we trust this man, Gabe?" Mom asked. See? I told you. She'd never trust a stranger no matter how friendly or shiny the fruit.

"I made a deal with him. His freedom for yours. He'll follow through, too. He's a bit of an emerging idealist. Just stick with him. He's got import/export connections that he's going to use. By this time tomorrow you'll be out of the states altogether."

"What do you mean 'YOU' Dad!?" I yelled, suddenly aware that Dad wasn't including himself in his pronouns.

"I'm going a different way out. I'm too high profile, right now. We'll meet up in South America."

Mom nodded, her eyes closed trying not to cry. Dad pulled her close. "You should have left me, Kathy." He whispered, but I heard. "You should have left me long ago."

Mom clung to him. "I don't understand..."

Dad pulled away slowly. "This might help." he said as he pulled a small envelop from his suit pocket. "It explains things a bit."

She nodded solemnly as she took it.

Next it was my turn for hugs. Dad snatched me up like I was a little girl again. "Everything that I've ever done that has hurt you has not been your fault at all." He cooed in my ear like a dove.

I couldn't stop crying.

"You are my girls and you are the world. You are what is worth having. I kept you both away because I couldn't drag you in. I wanted you safe. But I blew it." he whispered, lowering me. "Wherever you go, keep painting and drawing. And make sure that you get into trouble for it." He gave me a whole new smile I hadn't seen before. I'm sure I could draw it from memory as well as his other one.

We climbed into the boat, me still blubbering like a girl in a prom dress forgotten at the doorstep. Mom held me and we waved goodbye. Dad's arm went out once, palm open, fingers outstretched, figure tall. I drew him like that while on a plane a few days later.

On the boat I cried with my head in Mom's lap. Rosa clung onto Finny while she watched the water in the distance. Mom read Dad's letter while stroking my hair. Thomas spoke tersely in some Asian language over his radio while the boat rocked us all into a lullaby trance, speeding us toward another shore.

XXI

Gabriel Wall

UCMJ Investigative interview transcript of Witness E3 Gabriel Wall
Ft. Hood S3
Major Christina Harroway conducting
█████████ – Tuesday, 14:00

Major: Good afternoon, Private.

Private: Major.

Major: Please state your full name and age.

Private: Private Gabriel Ross Wall, 21 years old.

Major: We are meeting here this afternoon to discuss an incident that occurred on ████████ at ████████ ████ in a small townhome near ████████ ████████████████████ Are you familiar with this event?

Private: I am.

Major: What was the name of your Platoon officer?

Private: Second Lieutenant William Burr.

Major: Did he have any nicknames or call signs?

Private: Some people called him 'Socks.'

Major: How long had you been under his command prior to the day of the event?

Private: I was under Lt. Burr's command for about three months before-hand.

Major: Did Lt. Burr do anything or say anything that alerted you to mental instability.

Private: Yes.

Major: Such as?

Private: He cut himself with his combat knife on his thighs. He said it was decorative scarification. He also did it on his forearms and his shoulders. He··· he also was a rapist, and raped a number of local women during house searches.

Major: Did he act alone in the act of rape?

Private: No. Several of the platoonies helped or held down the victims or their children or husbands···

Major: Did he make the families watch?

Private: Sometimes.

Major: Did you participate?

Private: No.

Major: How did they respond to you declining?

Private: I told them I was impotent.

Major: Is that why they asked you to stand guard?

Private: Yes.

Major: Why did you not report this in the months leading up to the event in question?

Private: According to the chain of command, I would have had to report my complaint directly to Burr himself.
　　　　rustling of papers

Major: Alright, I'm going to ask you about the event specifically.

Private: Alright.

Major: What was your duty on that day, in that specific home?

Private: I was the third man in the entry stack. I breeched the door and suppressed any indigenous personnel.

Major: What indigenous personnel did you encounter?

Private: Two older women and a younger woman breastfeeding a baby.

Major: How long did it take to secure the site?

Private: Less than thirty seconds.

Major: Who began conversing with the breast feeding woman?

Private: I did. I told her in Spanish to lay on the ground with her baby between the two older women.

Major: Why did you do this? Lt. Burr was trained for search and questioning in Spanish, not you.

Private: I didn't want to let him see her breast out.

Major: Did she comply?

Private: No. She was angry. As were the other two women.

Major: What did they do?

Private: They yelled at me. Lt. Burr came up to them and tried to speak to them in Spanish.

Major: Did he follow the script?

Private: Yes, he followed the script. He tried to be polite, but his Spanish wasn't the greatest. They kept yelling over him.

Major: Is this when the escalation occurred?

Private: Yes. He started laughing, then grabbed the baby out of the younger woman's arms by the ankles.

Major: And?

Private: He held the baby high up over his head.

Major: What did the women do?

Private: They pleaded. They begged.
        silence

Major: Continue, Private.

Private: He then swung the baby into the wall, crushing its head.

Major: And the women?

Private: They cried, and he ordered us to lay them down, face down.

Major: Did you?

Private: Yes.

Major: What happened next?

Private: Lt. Burr swung the baby around like a church censer, saying he was blessing everyone.
Major: Did anyone say anything?
Private: No.
Major: Why not?
silence
Major: Private?
Private: According to the chain of command, I would have had to report my complaint directly to Burr himself.
Major: Set all that aside for a moment, Private. I want a serious answer. How did not one of you well-performing infantry men do anything?
silence
Major: A lot is riding on your answers here today, Private.
Private: I understand, Major.
silence
Private: What is there to say? I mean, we'd been kicking down doors and killing Mexicans for weeks. All of us knew we were going straight to hell. Even the chaplain did. Two days earlier four guys raped a nun, claiming it was to make her un-Catholic. You send us down there to quell government corruption and stop the gang war and then get angry at us when we become monsters?
Major: Your congress sent you down there. Sent US down there.
Private: Yeah, they send us just everywhere don't they?
Major: I don't think you are in the position to voice displeasure regarding your duties, soldier. This is an interview to ascertain if you should stand trial with many others in your platoon.
Private: I could give a fuck.
Major: Private⋯

Private: Like I said, I'm going to hell with the rest of them. No more wondering.

Major: Anything you say here can–

Private: Yeah I know. I also know that when I get home whenever that is, I'm going to see my two-year-old little girl and my wife and think about how she used to breast feed her in the kitchen at the table. **silence**

Private: Got kids, Major?

Major: PRIVATE.

Private: Breast feed them?

Major: This interview is now over.

Private: Know why I know that baby was a little girl? No one else knew it was a little girl, but I did. **silence**

Private: Because I bundled all four of their bodies together before we burned the place down. I at least wanted their bodies together.

Major: Private, I am going to place you in counseling.

Private: Whew, I'm saved.

Major: I'm also going to recommend demotion to E1.

Private: Swell. I loved CQ duty. That's, what, a two week setback?

Major: I am ordering a comprehensive psychological evaluation that will–

Private: No doubt find me fit enough to serve and then I'll be back out there, busting my way toward E4 again in no time. Let's not kid ourselves. Lt. Burr has been raping other soldiers for God's sake. His prior duty stations would call in advance to warn people about him off the record. **silence**

Private: The UCMJ and the Army only cares when it hits the news.

Major: Your Article 15 stands. You will be without pay
         while detained, and you will be assigned a
         representative from the UCMJ to protect your
         rights during the proceedings. Thank you for your
         time and co-operation, Private.
Private: Fuck you.

XXII

Lysander Nikoedemus

Not caring for the passage of time, I most likely slept for days. Given the stitches to my anus, I usually kept to lying on my side and staring at the frosted glass of a barred window on the farthest side of the infirmary.

I did not know what floor I was on, which wing I was in, what time it was, or what was to happen next. The drone of the infirmary lights had become my lullaby, and the occasional warm body of either a nurse or another injured prisoner was my only sign of other life on this planet.

A fellow prisoner had acted as my caretaker for the duration of my time in the infirmary. His yellowing fingernails glided along my sheets as he made my bed, and his steady, gnarled hands moved me from the bathroom and back to urinate. "Your bowels were cleared when they put you under for stitches." Was the only thing he had said to me, most likely anticipating my fears of a painful bowel movement.

I suspected he was a kind man, because he left a bible by my bedside. A real, non-federal bible from many years ago when the nation was secular. It was an unfamiliar translation, unmolested by either my government or my peers. Such publications are uncommon and discouraged, but the government never dared to ban The Book, although the printing of non-standard deviations is quietly forbidden.

"Where am I going to be transferred to?" I asked, knowing days had passed and I wasn't to stay in the solace of the infirmary forever. He looked me up and down as I sat on the toilet.

"You're in the heretic wing." he said flatly. "Better there. No real violent offenders. It's where they lock up all the men who worship the right man in the wrong way."

I nodded dully, and I was so overcome with relief, that I cried. Mormons and Jehovah Witnesses weren't typically a violent bunch by nature, and it occurred to me that I wouldn't be raped again the instant I returned to general population. They were often political prisoners more than anything, and I had heard tales of their banding together in and out of prison for protection and care.

I cried.

I cried because I was ashamed that I assumed I'd never experience rape. I presumed, as I suspect many men do, that it was a horror exclusive to the fairer sex and my thoughts on the crime would be limited to sympathy and distant rage. However here I was, violated and helpless. I am now forever a rape victim, and not as a child or a woman as expected, but as a grown man.

I cried because I wasn't mourning the death of an evil man, despite how my Christly heart said I should. I was supposed to lament the evils of men and pray for their souls as they surely faced suffering after death. Just as Luke wrote, I was supposed to merely turn the other check instead of finding comfort in the violent solution that ended my torment.

I cried because I was grateful for being saved by the very man who put me here. Gabriel Wall arrived, arm outstretched and pointed, and smote my enemy before me in a spectacular display of power. He moved men to kill with a motion, and not only did I benefit from it, I was glad that it had happened. My highest enemy is who I must now rely upon to survive. Much like Cray, keeping me as his pet for all to observe, will Wall also parade me as a show of his own strength?

I cried because I was humbled, and knew my passion was nothing in comparison to that of our savior. It was only my body, and it was only a brief period of time. I still had food and some level of safety. Christ starved in the desert, suffered manipulations from people, society, and the devil himself. He suffered betrayal. Christ gave up a chance to be a happy man, and his flesh was flayed from his body, his brow pierced with thorns, and his frame nailed to the cross that he had dragged through town. Yet I was so infinitely glad to be safe of it. I would have done anything or said anything to avoid a second brutal encounter with Cray. That man, with the tattooed image of Christ gazing wearily upward on his chest, would have plowed me into two pieces like a bloody, pulpy furrow.

As I wept, my caretaker's dark hand rested on my shoulder. Preventing me from teetering on the toilet, it was firm, but uncontrolling. He said nothing, but his being there was everything.

XXIII

Monsignor Michael Joseph Howell III

Ah, home again home again jiggety-jig! I have the high-rise flat in the Pembroke building that overlooks Arlington National Cemetery. To be honest, rising from your bed every morning to view the cemetery can be an encouraging way to start your day. I find it reassuring and invigorating, knowing that I am alive and well and have our nation's bedrock watching on.

Things all fit perfectly into plan and this just so happens to be one of those days where I am full to the brim with joy. You see, everything has fit into place as God would intend. Mueller, plagued with an over-developed sense of guilt, shot himself. He was a Godly man, but lacked the constitution required to make the hard choices as a leader and grasp the greater picture. When he shot himself, I know I wasn't the only one to secretly thank God.

It took no time at all for my boys to come up with an appropriate perpetrator, Albert Sergent. After sticking Gabriel onto his trail, it was only a matter of time before Sergent was found having bled to death in a Fairfax home. The family that walked in and found him will most likely benefit from their fifteen minutes of fame. I can't *wait* until tonight's news cast so I can see all the ugly details of Sergent's slow demise on the big screen. All the loose ends are coming together with several promising conspiracy threads to be unraveled by our best writers in The News and The Christendom Post, one of which even involves a pacifist preacher! Gabriel says he is innocent, but this Nikodemus fellow is a great opportunity to demonize bibliophiles. Better and better!

My home smells like tulips. All homes should smell like tulips.

The doorman greets me and Carla already has my dinner waiting for me at the table. My dining room set is actually Dutch imported and hand-crafted to match my Italian drapes. It makes for excellent conversation while entertaining guests and my guests deserve to dine on nothing less. The chair cushions are all white silk!

Ah, Carla has made her famous turkey. She's an amazing cook and a wonderful house maid and truly blessed by The Lord given her successful battle with cancer. I give my thanks to The Lord and His Son before I enjoy my meal. Bacon wrapped turkey is exactly what I need at the end of such a stressful day.

The common man is *so* out of touch with the bigger picture. It makes communicating to him what is best more and more difficult, especially in these stressful times. Sometimes I wonder why I bother or even try. And besides, today I had to say goodbye to a very dear friend. I will miss her. She was so wonderful but it was time to move on, and things were just getting too complicated. I had permitted her to lure me out of focus, and with all that is going on I simply must stay on God's task.

Each room in my home is decorated with a different theme. The smoking room has more of a rustic Western feel which I found suiting given the stone hearth fireplace. My oriental-themed lounge is finely decorated by couches of red cherry and jade accents. All three bathrooms have a Venetian charm via black marble and Spanish tile. And of course, my favorite room, is my art-deco office with Swarovski crystal doors. I'm currently working on a small museum room with some Sumerian and Byzantine pieces, mostly pre-iconoclastic, for the viewing pleasure of company whenever it may call. Which is often these days.

I've just taken my last bite when Trevor walks in.

"Sir, there's a power outage to the lower part of the building. Some of the security cameras and scanners are down. Could we have your permission to bring up several more guards for safety's sake?" he asks.

My apartment has a backup generator on the roof that can keep me in fine comfort for up to five months if power is lost. I also have a safe room behind the bedroom wall mirror that could keep me fed and well-kept for nearly a year. Gabriel designed my entire security and defense system from the ground up. My very own angel of death. I list the names of five guards that I approve of, and Trevor walks out. I picked ones that Gabriel assigned to the post himself.

People have been high-strung since the "assassination" of Charles Mueller. Ha!

Refilling my wine glass, I stand. Around this time I retire to the lounge and make whatever phone calls are required for the day. As I prepare to do so I hear a loud boom in the distance and the picture frames rattle for a moment. Car alarms chirp. Carla comes running in, saying something, while pointing out the window. She and I stand side by side looking down at the street eight stories below us at what looks to be a fire. I ask Carla to get the radio so that I can talk to the guards.

I wonder if it's a gas main. If it is, I know exactly who to call tomorrow morning. I met the utility commissioner at a party last March and he was a kind enough fellow, well-mannered and God fearing. He and I got on well and it would be a good chance for me to call him and catch up. Maybe he'd do me a favor or two given a gas line of his exploded right under my home.

Goodness. I hope no one was hurt.

Carla hands me the radio. I speak into it, calling down to the gate. No one answers. I try again. Still no response. The front door opens in the distance and I hear footsteps rushing through the halls toward Carla and me. I call out, announcing that everything is fine and that we're unhurt. These men can be jumpy.

Trevor looks white. "We need to get you to the emergency elevator, sir! We need to leave *now!*" He has three other men behind him, all with pistols out. I'm thinking of how I can talk sense into this poor young man when everything goes white and my ears are suddenly ringing with pain! I don't know where up or down is and my balance is gone! I grab onto Carla, using her to hold myself up. After a few moments my vision returns and I can slowly hear again. It's gunfire! WHO'S SHOOTING IN MY HOME!? Trevor's on his knees firing his pistol into my walls and two of the other men are on the ground. The third man is performing CPR, his hands covered in blood. I can now hear Carla's screaming and a whistling of wind behind me. Turning around I see that there are bullet holes in my window. Bullet holes!

Someone's yelling at me, telling me to get down. I turn back around to see the man performing CPR yelling at me. As he's doing so, something red pops at the top of his head and he falls asleep instantly. I try shaking him, but he's not waking up.

"He's dead!" Trevor yells, grabbing my arm and yanking on me. It hurt! And he's dead? How did he die?

What's going on!? Am I under attack!? Is someone after me!?

"I don't know!" Trevor yells, dragging me down a hallway to my bedroom. He fires his pistol blindly behind us as we run. I ask about Carla. He doesn't seem to care. Opening the safe room, he shoves me inside. Isn't he coming in?

No, he stands strong and protective as the door closes between us. God, please protect Trevor. Please watch over him and his eternal soul.

I've never been in the safe room before. It's completely dark and I can't see anything. My hearing is nearly back to normal now, but despite my straining I can't hear what's going on outside. Maybe the walls are too thick. Taking a deep breath, I calm myself, and thank The Lord for delivering me to safety. I begin feeling around for a light switch.

"It's started. I'm starting it. And you're the first one against the wall." someone says. The lights come on, and it's Gabriel. Thank you, God! I'm saved! He's even dressed in all black combat gear with a blast vest, his face painted and covered with a balaclava ready for the emergency at hand. His eyes absolutely glow, and they glow at me.

Thank God Gabriel is here. Now, what do we do? Is more help on the way? How did he know of the attack? What did he say? What... against the wall? How am I against the wall? What's starting? I-I don't understand. Gabe? What are

About the Cover Artist

Sorin Michalski is an unusual anomaly from my high school days back in Florida. He was peculiar in that he was insanely popular, handsome, brilliant, and despite all of those factors he did NOT beat me up on a daily basis. Heck, he didn't even get around to beating my scrawny ass on a *weekly* basis. No, Sorin was an oddity in that he was the full package; sharp, talented, well natured, and he looked smashing in drag.

Figure a: many of us couldn't figure if he was hotter as a girl or a guy

After my army discharge/divorce/homelessness was pretty much through, I set out to see if my classmates had failed as completely at life as I had. Lo and behold, I found Sorin and the catastrafuck that was his existence made me infinitely grateful.

Figure b: the poor bastard

At some point I called Sorin to do the cover for my second novel. I suspect that he set down his martini reluctantly, patted his two genetically perfect sons on the head as he walked passed them, and answered the phone at a tiki bar. I had to explain who I was to some extent. What jarred his memory loose was 'Magic the Gathering' combined with 'wore only black denim' and he remembered me.

"I think I ran by you several times when we did the mile in gym." He said.

As it turns out, Sorin had taken to being an activist. The sunny beaches and surf of California had fostered his sense of social justice into a full-on fungal bloom and he had spent years networking to the effect of making the world a better place. Sorin had harnessed social media, guerilla art, and the literary world to a noble end. He never said as much, but I suspect that he wanted a better world for his sons to grow up in. That, and Sorin always was a bit of a rebel.

Sorin not only was eager to read Withered Zion immediately, he actually did so! The man gobbled the novel up, instantly chatted with me over the phone regarding it, and then began making preliminary designs for the cover art. Despite the demands he could have made of me regarding payment or working methods, he made none. He wanted to serve the novel and please *me*.

Figure c: off is the general direction in which The Man can kindly *FUCK*

And please me he did, but he scared me as well. Unlike my outings with previous artists, he was fairly secretive to his creative process. Art is an intimate affair for Sorin, and despite his outward and confident nature, his process of creation suddenly revealed his vulnerabilities. When I told him I adored being in on every paint stroke of my cover-creation, he shyly stated 'I um, I don't work like that, really.' Despite still being assertive, it was the only time this shift in his voice occurred. I knew to back off instantly.

In the end, he mailed the piece off to me without even showing me a picture of the finished product! I was gnawing my nails off in anticipation! What if it sucked!? What if I couldn't make sense of it!? What if it was so far beyond the novel in quality and brilliance that my own creation was outshined entirely!?

I promised him I'd call him the moment I got it, and indeed I did. Pocket knife out, I tore into that package like a kid at Christmas. Several slices later, and with the living room covered in packaging material, I held it up into the sunlight. I dialed Sorin, got him on the phone, and he didn't even wait for me to say hello.

"What do you think, man?"

"It looks like something Michelle Bachman would mount on her bedroom ceiling so that her effeminate husband can bring her to climax." was the first sentence I could muster.

Between chuckles, Sorin confessed that he had never gotten a compliment like that before. I hope he puts it on his business card.

What struck me most about his artwork was the combination of subtly and thematic that he employed. He connected with the metaphor behind Lysander's rape significantly, noticing how the man decorated with Christ's suffering only felt Jesus on a superficial level. Cray's skin-deep faith and his brutal rape of the devout Lysander was an attempt to destroy holiness in another. In a nutshell, that scene was a microcosm for the entire novel and Sorin snatched it up instantly.

"I collected Christian tattoos. Check em out. They are all over the cover, dude."

Figure d: Nothing proves one's devotion to Christ faster and more irrefutably than a weeping Jesus tramp-stamp.

He brought my novel to life, which left me with an unforeseen challenge that I have yet to even address... where the hell do I sell this thing!? Who would buy it!? The cover looks like Bill O'Reilly's wet dream but surely he'd only get a few pages into it before he caught onto me. I'm entirely at fault for writing a novel that is nearly unsellable, but in the end I couldn't be happier with the cover. It reflects the book perfectly, and given that it was produced by an accomplished West Coast artist (insert shout-out for West Side *here* with random palsy-inspired gang gesture) I've got some muscle in my corner.

I regret not spending more time with Sorin in high school, now. I should not have been so intimidated and jealous of his being everything I wasn't. The man is polite, kind natured, and genuine in a refreshing manner that makes me feel warmly welcomed and unjudged. He brought my meditation on America's flirtations with Christo-fascism to life vibrantly and elegantly. I wonder what he brings to life in others, and what he might have brought to life for me if I had only stopped playing Magic the Gathering for a few damned minutes.

If you want Sorin Michalski to bring something of YOURS to life, check him out at www.groundupart.com and also hit him up on his very active facebook page. He'll be easy to find since NO ONE ON THIS EARTH has been previously named 'Sorin Michalski!'

For Ginger, my Christian

Edited by Shaun Carres, Amanda Mercer, Todd Bell, Jan Montgomery, Paul Page and Abigail Page. Blame them for typos!

Made in the USA
Charleston, SC
05 September 2014